# The Mask on the Cruise Ship

## Melanie Jackson

ORCA BOOK PUBLISHERS

# Praise for the
# Dinah Galloway Mysteries:

"...fun and witty...delightful characters...for mystery lovers everywhere!" —*Resource Links*

"With writing as delicious as the fresh tomatoes Dinah loves to munch, Jackson weaves a lively mystery. The book is often hilarious, but touches on serious themes." —*Quill & Quire*

"...engaging and highly readable...a fast-paced tale that keeps the reader guessing until the end." —*Vancouver Sun*

"Jackson spares no artistic expense in either *The Spy in the Alley* or *The Man in the Moonstone*, both of which are set in Vancouver's East Side. She knows how to write a full-bodied scene, gauges correctly that it's worth her time to drolly title her chapters ("Sour notes with Piano Man"), crafts worthy subplots, and delivers strong characterizations of even second-banana players." —*The Horn Book*

**National Library of Canada Cataloguing in Publication Data:**

Jackson, Melanie, 1956-
The mask on the cruise ship / Melanie Jackson.

(A Dinah Galloway mystery)
ISBN 1-55143-305-2

I. Title. II. Series: Jackson, Melanie, 1956- . Dinah Galloway mystery.

PS8569.A265M38 2004            jC813'.6            C2004-905221-7

**Library of Congress Control Number:** 2004112464

**Summary:** As the ship-board entertainment on an Alaska-bound cruiseship,
twelve-year-old Dinah Galloway is on the trail of a stolen Native artifact.

Orca Book Publishers gratefully acknowledges the support for its publishing programs provided by the following agencies: the Government of Canada
through the Department of Canadian Heritage's Book Publishing Industry
Development Program (BPIDP), the Canada Council for the Arts, and the
British Columbia Arts Council.

Typesetting by Lynn O'Rourke
Raven Mask Image: Leonard Joseph, Raven Mask,
Collection of John and Ann Miller
photography courtesy of Kentucky Museum of Art and Craft

**In Canada:**                           **In the United States:**
Orca Book Publishers                  Orca Book Publishers
Box 5626, Stn B.                      PO Box 468
Victoria, BC Canada                   Custer, WA USA
V8R 6S4                               98240-0468

08 07 06 05 • 6 5 4 3 2
Printed and bound in Canada

*To Bart and Sarah-Nelle Jackson*

With thanks to:
My editor, Andrew Wooldridge, for giving
Dinah her chance in the limelight

My former boss, Shelley Fralic of the
*Vancouver Sun*, for permitting me to adapt
information from her May 2001 series on her
own Alaska cruise

My friend Ruby Best, for helping me with
Dinah's website,
http://www3.telus.net/dinah/spy.htm

# Table of Contents

# Chapter 1

*Mr. Trotter ought to relax*

To me, it resembled a fat white bar of soap.

"Oooo, yes. Our lovely *Empress Marie*," gushed Mr. Trotter, program director for Happy Escapes Cruise Lines. He'd scurried over to stand beside me at the office tower window. Far below us, in the blue-green waters of Vancouver's inner harbor, the fat white bar of soap—er, the *Empress Marie*—gleamed in the May sunshine.

Mr. Trotter clasped his hands beneath his chin. "You're such a fortunate young woman, Dinah Galloway. Imagine—performing on one of our ships at your tender age and experience!"

Sighing, he raised his eyes to the ceiling, his round, apple-red cheeks glowing over his curled and waxed mustache.

"I'm twelve-and-a-third, and my experience is nothing to sneeze at," I objected. I opened my mouth again to continue my comments at some length. Namely, that I sang in radio commercials for Sol's Salami on West Fourth: *Pastrami, Baloney, Not An Ounce That's Phony!*

It was a great song, which I loved belting out, and Sol gave my mother, my sister and me tons of free samples. Num.

Plus, I'd been in a play last November. A musical, *The Moonstone*. "This freckle-faced, red-haired kid sang her heart out — and stole mine," a critic wrote. Not bad, huh?

But a frown from my agent, sitting by Mr. Trotter's desk, stopped me from explaining all this. Dignified, iron-gray-haired Mr. Wellman had advised me to stay fairly mum at our meeting with the program director. To squash my personality. "I love your enthusiasm for life," Mr. Wellman had assured me. "Mr. Trotter, though, is the nervous type. If the slightest thing about a performer upsets him, he won't sign them for a Happy Escapes cruise."

And I did want to go. A cruise to Alaska and back, the first one of the season! The chance had come up because one of the performers who'd already been booked, a china-cup juggler, had backed out. Mother and Madge would go with me, we'd see fjords and glaciers, and there'd be food, *food*, FOOD. I beamed at Mr. Trotter.

matter what my bloopers. My bared-teeth smile relaxed into a real one.

"Another room..." Mr. Trotter patted his mustache nervously. "But I'm not sure about Miss Galloway..."

"You're lucky, on such short notice, to get a talent like Dinah," my agent reminded him. Then Mr. Wellman shrugged. "Still, if you're not interested – "

"Wait," the program director protested. Perhaps he was reflecting that a loudmouth pre-teen who showed up for work was, after all, more reliable than a china-cup juggler who didn't. "Another room," he said again, only in a much friendlier tone. "One where the young lady wouldn't be *with* us...ye-es...Come along, Dinah."

Mr. Wellman winked at me. I got up and followed the ever-scurrying program director to a door behind his desk. He opened it to reveal a cozy room with sofas, a coffee table and a TV. And, through one wall of sheer glass, another drop-dead stunning view of Vancouver's sparkling harbor and the blue-violet mountains looming beyond.

Mr. Trotter gave each of his mustache curls a nudge upward in case they were drooping. "Enjoy!" he said, with false jolliness. I had a feeling he wasn't over my remarks about his shortness. "Oh, and I always keep treats in here for my guests. Help yourself! Enjoy!"

*Slam.*

Nope. He wasn't over the shortness thing.

**I stood on my** toes and stretched my arms as high as they would go. I sure wished I would get taller. I saw my reflection in the glass and thought, Face it. You're a Madge wannabe.

But how many girls could look like Madge? With her creamy skin, burnished red hair and vivid blue eyes, Madge had once earned lots of money modeling.

That was before she'd decided modeling was too shallow and she'd rather concentrate on drawing and painting.

I grimaced at my freckled, bespectacled self in the window. In my opinion, you had to be pretty, like Madge, in order to dismiss an emphasis on appearance as being shallow.

And why couldn't *my* hair be a burnished red? It was more of a washed-out red, like a Canadian flag that had been laundered once too often.

Oh well. That was the advantage of keeping one's hair messy, I decided. The color wasn't so noticeable.

Shrugging, I shifted my gaze to the coffee table. Ah. Food. The treats Mr. Trotter had mentioned. Some mints in a bowl, a box of chocolates and — hmmm. A Styrofoam container.

Inside the container was, num!, a huge egg salad sandwich. Now, I should be clear about this. My favorite sandwich, bar none, is banana–peanut-butter–honey. But I wasn't about to complain. This mega-sandwich, in thick sourdough bread, was crammed with pickles, tomatoes, onions, green peppers and lettuce. I was practically swooning as I chomped.

Farther along the coffee table, some files were stacked. Paper-clipped to the top file was a scribbled note on Happy Escapes Cruise Lines stationery — deep blue, with a drawing of a fat white ship in the upper left corner.

I always like to read when I eat alone, so I picked up the note.

*Mr. Trotter —*
*Borrowed the contents of this for a while. Hope you don't mind.*
                                                    *— Peabody Roberts*

I checked the top file, which was labeled "*Empress Marie* Passenger List." Empty. I tossed note and file back on the table. *That* certainly hadn't been interesting reading.

I was just licking the last bit of egg salad off my fingers when the door opened. Mr. Trotter had his hand on the knob, but in response to something Mr. Wellman had said he was looking back over his shoulder. I sat up straight, prepared to thank him very nicely for the sandwich.

"No, thank you, I won't join you and Dinah for lunch," the program director called back cheerily to Mr. Wellman. "Today I'm treating myself to my favorite sandwich — egg salad with all the trimmings — from the deli downstairs. I appreciate the invitation, but I've been anticipating this scrumptious delight all morning. Really," and here he giggled, "I've been counting the minutes till I take that first, heavenly bite."

OH NO. In panic I eyed the now-empty Styrofoam container. Why hadn't Mr. Trotter explained to me that the "treats" he kept in here for his guests didn't include sandwiches?

"I'm so glad you've decided on Dinah," Mr. Wellman was saying. "You won't be sorry."

Mr. Trotter wagged a playful finger. "So long as there are no disruptions, Wellman. No disturbances. I value calm above all else."

This was awful. There wouldn't be a shred of calm left to Mr. Trotter once he discovered his lunch was missing. In fact, the only shreds would be my contract — after he'd ripped it up. No Alaska cruise for Mother, Madge and me.

Gulp. My palms were now so clammy that the *Empress Marie* could've just about floated in them. Then —

I noticed again the note that was paper-clipped to the top file.

*Mr. Trotter —*
*Borrowed the contents of this for a while. Hope you don't mind.*

*— Peabody Roberts*

After a last giggle at some remark of Mr. Wellman's, the program director started to turn.

I grabbed the note, slapped it on top of the Styrofoam container and weighed it down with the paper clip.

"Come back in and join us, my dear," smiled Mr. Trotter.

"We're all done... Hope you helped yourself to some chocolates."

"Um," I said, but Mr. Trotter wasn't listening. He was patting his mustache curls, I guess to make sure the smile hadn't dislodged them in any way.

**Mr. Wellman and** I waited at the elevator.

"You'll love the cruise," he assured me. "I know someone else who's going: Julie Hébert. Julie's the stepsister of a client of mine, Professor Elaine Hébert, a renowned expert in First Nations culture. I book speeches and TV appearances for Professor Hébert.

"Anyhow, the prof's sister will be transporting a valuable Tlingit Nation mask to an art gallery in Juneau."

"Hey, we studied Tlingit masks this year," I exclaimed. "Shamans, who were people with special powers, put masks on to drive evil away. Ravens, eagles and other animals were the spiritual helpers the shamans called on. When the shaman wore a mask of one of these animals, it meant the animal was right there, helping him."

I flapped my arms and ran back and forth in front of the elevators. I thought it'd be exciting to be a shaman, able to battle the dark spirits.

"Er, Dinah." Mr. Wellman caught me by an arm. "Maybe you should come in for a landing. Remember, Lionel Trotter is into *soothing* surroundings."

"Oh, right," I said and stopped flapping. "So what's with the mask that's going on the *Empress Marie*?"

"Professor Hébert had borrowed the mask for an exhibition at the University of British Columbia. She was planning to return it herself, but then she got invited on an archeological dig in northern B.C. So the prof gave the cruise ticket to her stepsister."

"Lucky Julie," I commented.

"Not so lucky," Mr. Wellman said thoughtfully. "There's been something rather sinister — "

However, I wasn't to find out about Julie and the sinister something just yet. Mr. Trotter burst out of his office into the hallway. His apple cheeks had reddened to a dark beet color. He was quivering so much with indignation that his thick mustache curls were dancing, like the "Waltz of the Flowers" scene in the *Nutcracker* ballet.

Talk about being possessed by evil spirits. Mr. Trotter, I thought, could have used a shaman himself about now. He bellowed at the receptionist: "WHERE IS PEABODY? I'M GOING TO TAKE HIM APART LIMB BY LIMB!"

# Chapter 2
## The Raven and the stepsister

Julie Hébert lifted the box's lid. A scarlet flame jutted out at us.

I grinned.

Mother jumped.

Madge, who loved using bright, bold colors in her art, smiled delightedly. "It's a beak, Mother," she exclaimed. "It's..."

"It's the Raven," I said, as Julie drew the bubble wrap away from the fierce, vivid mask. "He's in so many First Nations legends, but my favorite is the one where he captures the light."

"Me, too," nodded Julie, whom Mr. Wellman had brought by to meet us. "When the Raven wants something, nothing stops him."

My friend Pantelli Audia and I had done a project on the Raven for school. According to legend, in the beginning the whole world was dark. A rich man and his daughter selfishly hoarded all stars, the moon and the sun in three bags hanging on their wall.

The curious, bright-eyed Raven decided enough was enough. Time to let the light free to shine on everyone. He changed himself into a pine needle that the girl swallowed when drinking a cup of water.

As well as selfish, the girl must've been awfully stupid, I figured. Imagine not noticing that you'd gulped back a pine needle!

The pine needle part was Pantelli's favorite. Pantelli loves trees. He wants to be a tree doctor when he grows up, or maybe a forest ranger. So, for our project, he went into a five-page rant about different types of pine needles—how it must've been a needle from the dwarf pine that the girl swallowed, as opposed to one from a regular-sized pine.

We got points taken off, needless—or should that be needles?—to say. OFF TOPIC, the teacher wrote scornfully.

Back to the myth of the Raven. Having been digested by the girl, he changed himself into a baby, which she then gave birth to.

The baby/Raven started crying nonstop. I guess there weren't any pacifiers in those far-off mythic days. The girl and her dad shoved the bags at the baby to keep him quiet. Dumb-dee-dumb-dumb. The baby/Raven opened the bags, probably with a big, gleeful *caw!*, and let loose the stars, moon and sun.

I studied the Raven's long beak, with its red rim stretching like a smile. And the round black eyes, alert and—humorous, I thought.

"He's funny," I said.

Julie nodded, pleased. "You're right, Dinah. The Raven has an excellent sense of humor. I've always thought that's the source of his cunning, his mischief, in all the stories about him."

"As long as he doesn't use his mischief for ill," murmured Mother—a typical no-fun, Motherly comment, I thought and shook my head at her. She was so embarrassing sometimes.

Julie stroked the bright red beak. "The Raven's challenge is to turn his gift of mischief to good use. He doesn't always succeed. I think that if you were that clever, that capable of fooling others, it would be very hard to stay on the straight and narrow all the time."

Madge was still gazing, entranced, at the mask. Like me, she was too much in awe of the Raven to care about his off days. "Since he brought light to the world, I think we pretty much have to forgive him everything," she pointed out.

"With fans like you, the guy definitely doesn't need an agent," remarked Mr. Wellman. "Hey, Julie, you're really knowledgeable. Maybe *you* should start giving lectures on the Raven."

"I'd be at every one," promised Madge, who was starting at Emily Carr Institute of Art in the fall. Her blue eyes shone.

Julie's round, cheery face began to rival the Raven's for redness, only it was embarrassment, not ferocity. "I don't think Elaine would approve," she said, running a hand through her spiky-cut black hair. "She'd think I was shoving my way into the limelight."

"What's wrong with that?" I demanded. "I do that myself, as often as possible."

Julie hesitated. "You see, Elaine believes that amateurs should keep quiet. She says it took her years to become a professor, so she's earned the right to be a public figure. Whereas someone like me—well, I love art and mythology, and I'm actually an artist, too. Or trying to be! But I don't have a fancy Ph.D. like Elaine."

"P-h-*phooey*," I said, deciding I didn't like this sister of Julie's very much. Sounded like Elaine put on quite the airs.

Julie ran her hand through her hair again. She was one of those people with untidy hair that looked chic and expensive, whereas mine just looked untidy.

She confided, "Besides, with what's been happening, I'd rather keep a lowered profile on the cruise."

Julie had quieted her voice even beyond its usual softness. I leaned forward to be able to hear her. Unfortunately, my cat-slippered toes crunched on some bubble wrap that had fallen. *Pop, pop, pop!*

"We don't need sound effects, Dinah," Madge reprimanded. Being dreamy, she was pretty quiet and soft-spoken herself.

"Sorry," I apologized. Nope, I just wasn't the type to maintain a soothing atmosphere.

Julie was more twinkly-eyed than offended, so I plunged on, full of curiosity. "Mr. Wellman mentioned a sinister something. Is it to do with the mask?"

Julie nodded. "Someone's been trying to steal it."

Madge and Mother also leaned forward to hear. Hunched in a circle around Julie, the three of us resembled cloves of garlic.

**There'd been two** attempts to steal the mask, Julie explained.

The first had been at her apartment on Cadwallader Avenue, where she'd stored the Raven initially. Someone had climbed the tree next to her second-story window, slid along the nearest branch, jimmied the window open—

And crashed to the ground when the branch broke beneath him.

"The police deduce that it was a 'he' from the footprints limping away from the scene," Julie explained. "A man of slight build, about five nine."

Mother broke in with a Motherly *tsk*. "Cadwallader's not the best area for a young woman to be living in. So much crime! It's not safe for you, let alone the Raven, Julie."

Julie shrugged. "It's all I can afford, at least till my paintings sell. An art dealer told me I had real talent—that it wouldn't be long till I could hold a show in his gallery!"

Finding out about the attempted theft, Elaine insisted Julie bring the mask to her beautiful house in the Shaughnessy area. Julie could stay there with the mask until the cruise; Elaine herself was already off on her archeological dig.

For the privilege of staying at Elaine's, Julie had to scrub the house from top to bottom. "I don't mind, though," Julie assured us.

Mother, Madge and I exchanged looks. So Julie was stuck on grimy Cadwallader Avenue while Elaine lived in swishy Shaughnessy! The only small houses there were the bird feeders. You'd think Elaine could spare Julie a teeny room at her place, at least while Julie struggled to make it as an artist.

Soon after Julie moved into Elaine's, the security alarm blared forth. Poking his head out, a neighbor saw a slight, medium-height man in black cap, sweat suit and black mask hobbling off. Obviously the same guy who'd tried breaking into her apartment. This time the burglar had taken fright at the alarm's loud pealing.

Mother and Madge looked horrified, but I had to stifle a laugh. The burglar's efforts reminded me of a Roadrunner cartoon. "It doesn't sound like we're dealing with an overly high IQ here," I observed.

"There's a big illegal market for art—a problem we should take very seriously," Mr. Wellman said. "Most likely some unsavory art dealer has hired our low-IQ thief. That's the police's theory, anyhow."

He told Julie, "One reason I wanted to introduce you to Dinah is that she's very observant, a natural detective. She'll watch out for you. In any case, once you set foot on the *Empress*, you'll be out of our thief's reach. Smooth sailing, I'd say." Mr. Wellman beamed at his little joke.

Madge, Mother and Julie laughed politely, but I took the opportunity to frown at him. Grown-ups were so bad at humor, in my view. Best not to encourage them.

**The adults started** talking about the luggage limit you could take on board a cruise ship. Mind-numbing. I mean, as long as I remembered to bring my CD player and Judy Garland and Bessie Smith CDs, I'd be well-equipped.

Excusing myself, I started to head upstairs. Then, in the front hall, "The Yellow Rose of Texas" tinkled out.

Either there was an elf-sized orchestra nearby or—yup. Somebody'd left a cell phone, a silver metallic one, on the hall table. I grabbed it.

"Hello?" I said.

Now, since I'd never seen the cell phone before, I knew quite well the call couldn't be for me. However, like the

Raven, I was naturally curious. Curiosity was my strong or weak point, depending on how you looked at it.

A female voice on the other end snapped, "Are you cleaning?"

"Not if I can help it," I replied in surprise.

A wail. "C'mon, you're staying in my house, aren't you? It needs cleaning. So get to work!"

This must be Julie's cell phone, and the woman on the other end must be—

"Elaine?" I guessed.

"Of course it's Elaine," Professor Hébert barked. "You listen to me, Julie. Take good care of the mask. Don't botch this for me. And don't talk to people about the Raven, or anything else for that matter! You're not the know-it-all you think you are. In fact, you know nothing! You're just a silly little—"

I scraped what little fingernails I owned over the mouthpiece. Nothing wrong with creating a little static. What a creep this Elaine was! It was surprising Julie had any self-confidence left at all.

"Sorry, can't hear you," I said and powered off.

# Chapter 3
## *Attack of the brussels sprouts*

Mother insisted Mr. Wellman and Julie stay for dinner. She asked Mr. Wellman if he'd like to phone his wife and invite her, too, but it turned out she was visiting friends in San Diego. "So you've saved me from a frozen dinner," my agent thanked Mother. "And, given my kitchen comprehension skills, frozen dinners tend to remain frozen, even after I've heated them up."

"Oh dear," fretted Mother, not recognizing yet another of Mr. Wellman's lame jokes. Like Madge, she was pretty, though in a softened, middle-aged kind of way, and dreamy to the point of being somewhat dotty. "How hungry you must be, then!...And you, Julie, is there anyone, um, a partner or family member you'd like to call—"

"Thanks, but I'm alone in the world except for my stepsister," Julie smiled. "And I don't see her much; she's so busy with her teaching and public speaking."

And with being nasty, I thought. I didn't tell Julie about Elaine's call. I was sure Julie got enough of her stepsister as it was.

Pantelli dropped by in time to join us for dinner, something he did often. Pantelli had already eaten, but, like mine, his appetite was endless. Unlike me, irritatingly, he stayed as skinny as the twigs he liked to examine through his magnifying glass.

He immediately applied the magnifying glass to the Raven. "Cool," he breathed.

"Yes, the mask combines the Raven's mischief and majesty all at once," Julie said.

Pantelli looked up, his brown eyes puzzled beneath his untidy black curls. "Huh? I meant the *wood*," he clarified. "It's yellow cedar. Very resistant to decay. Interestingly, the inner side of a yellow cedar's bark smells like potatoes."

"Er...speaking of potatoes, why don't we have some," Mother suggested to Julie, who seemed rather baffled. Pantelli took some getting used to. Like, years.

Over roast beef, garlic mashed potatoes and, much less pleasantly, brussels sprouts, Julie told us how she'd once visited a lecture of Elaine's.

"It was at the Vancouver Roundhouse Community Center. I tried to slip into the lecture room unseen — and knocked over a chair. Unluckily, Elaine had stacked books and papers on the chair. These went flying! What a commotion.

"Elaine was furious. Claimed I'd deliberately ruined the speech she was giving to these high school kids."

"Wow," said Pantelli. "You sound like Dinah. Impossible for Di to make a quiet entrance."

"I'm sure the lecture wasn't ruined," Mother reassured her as I glared at Pantelli. "Here, have some brussels sprouts, Dinah," and she ladled a mini-mountain of them onto my plate.

Mother then politely concentrated on Julie, who began talking about her art. These brussels sprouts have to go, I was thinking. I tipped my plate, emptying the mini-mountain into the napkin on my lap.

Madge eyed me with distaste. She was the type who took a good helping of vegetables and only dainty portions of mashed potatoes and beef. Sick, in my view. "Sometimes it's not only *step*sisters who are vastly, even frighteningly, different," she remarked.

This got her odd looks from Mother, Julie, Mr. Wellman and Pantelli, but I didn't think Madge was planning to give me away. Madge didn't tattletale when she was in a good mood.

Which she was, this week, because a) she was going on a cruise ship packed with clothing boutiques, and b) even better, Mr. Wellman had wangled a job for her boyfriend, Jack French, on the *Empress Marie* as a swimming instructor.

Jack was very athletic, with all kinds of Red Cross and Royal This-And-That badges and certificates. A regrettable side to an otherwise nice guy.

I'd guessed right about my sister, for, glowing with girlfriendly pride, she began to tell Julie about Jack: "He took a year off after high school to volunteer with an anti-smoking group, but this fall he starts university. He plans to become a teacher."

The rest of us smiled encouragingly. My smile was my phony, bared-teeth one, though. Not that I didn't admire Jack. I did, wholeheartedly.

However, my mind was on getting rid of the brussels sprouts.

**Rolling up the** brussels sprouts-stuffed napkin, I tucked it under my arm and mumbled an excuse about needing to go to the washroom. No one batted an eye. Smooth, or what?

I was being honest. I did need a washroom—so I could flush the sprouts down the toilet. If the yechy green things were so nutritious, let the city sewers be healthy.

By the upstairs bathroom, I paused to unroll the napkin. Beside me was Madge's room; the door to her balcony, which faced on to the street, was open. Madge had been leaving it open, even in the chilliest weather, since reading in one of her fashion magazines that too much indoor air stifled the complexion.

Right.

Now, through the balcony door, I heard a boy's voice say: "Yup, LOUD is the word for Dinah Galloway."

Huh? Still clutching the brussels sprouts-filled napkin, I went through Madge's room to the balcony and stepped out. The balcony railing was covered with wisteria that we let grow wild, much to our neighbors' disapproval. The advantage to us was that all those rampant leaves acted as a privacy screen.

Crouching below the railing, I peered through the leaves at the boy who'd just dissed me.

It was the new boy in my grade seven class. Talbot St. John.

There's a twerpy name for you. Imagine naming a kid "Talbot" if he was already stuck with "St. John."

The twerpish sound of it had not, however, prevented several girls in my class from going gaga over him. I suppose because he was tall—well, tall for a grade seven—with dark hair that drooped in a soulful lock over deep blue eyes.

Maybe it was the late-birthday thing again, but, soulful lock or not, I failed to understand why the girls stood around at recess in limp clumps, drained of any energy, and certainly of any personality, gazing with hopeless adoration at him.

It was one of the gaga girls he was talking to on the sidewalk: Liesl Dubuque, our neighbors' niece. Liesl was staying with them for a year while her parents traveled.

Liesl had a white, sharp face framed by wedge-cut black hair. She was always tugging on the back of her hair, the wedge part. I'd overheard her say she wanted to grow her hair out to—get this—impress Talbot.

As well as sharp features, Liesl had a sharp, scornful laugh, which she erupted into now.

"'LOUD' doesn't express it, Talbot. When Dinah opens her mouth, there's no point in anyone else trying to speak. Ms. Boom-Boom deafens us all."

"Talk about breaking the sound barrier," Talbot began—and Liesl's laugh sliced through the air again.

I'd had enough. Grabbing brussels sprouts, I started hurling them at the sidewalk duo. I had good aim, too, so—*splat! splat!*—the round green blobs smashed against their heads.

"AT LEAST I HAVE A PERSONALITY, YOU TWO TWERPS," I bellowed. "THEY'D HAVE TO SEND OUT A SEARCH PARTY TO FIND *YOURS*!"

Down to one brussels sprout, I crouched behind the wisteria-thick railing again. After all, you never knew. Talbot and Liesl might be packing eggs or tomatoes.

It was then that I noticed something.

Wisteria wasn't all that was gripping the balcony rails. At the side, two black-gloved hands were as well.

My mouth dropped into an elongated O. Amid the wisteria leaves, a black-balaclava-covered face stared back at me. I was able, at least, to see the eyes. They were a pale, and at this moment rather shocked, gooseberry color.

A burglar! He'd climbed the wisteria-laden trellis. He'd intended to break in by way of the balcony.

If I thought *my* jaw had plummeted, his had practically hit Australia. Frantic ideas about screaming or running for help fled my mind. I knew exactly what to do.

I took the last brussels sprout and shoved it through the railing into his wide-open mouth.

**Wrenching away in** reaction to the brussels sprout, the masked man yanked too hard on the trellis. Along with the sound of splitting wood, there was an "AAAGGH!" as the man fell back, back...into one of the firs separating our yard from the neighbors'.

I saw the man was dressed head-to-toe in black, including turtleneck, pants and hiking boots.

The evergreen he smashed backward against buckled under his weight. Then the tree trampolined him forward again. He slid straight down to thump in a painful heap on Mother's snapdragons.

There were voices behind me, on the stairs.

"What the—?" Mr. Wellman erupted.

"Property destruction?" came Pantelli's admiring voice. "Cool, Dinah."

From Mother, in an apologetic tone to Julie, "Somehow a household with Dinah in it is never quiet, if you know what I mean."

"It's not my fault," I objected, as the others joined me on the balcony. I pointed to the masked man, who was picking himself up with difficulty from the flattened snapdragons. "Bet it's your inept thief again, Julie."

Julie could only moan.

Deciding to be a bit more practical, I started to charge downstairs after the thief—but Mother and Madge held me back. "No tangling with criminals," Mother warned. "We leave on our cruise tomorrow."

Mr. Wellman punched in 911 on his cell phone. He had to plug a finger into his free ear and retreat inside the house to make the call, though, because at that moment our beefy neighbor stomped outside.

"WHO'S BEEN ATTACKING MY TREE?" yelled Liesl's uncle, Mr. Dubuque. He waved a hairy, white-knuckled fist at the fir tree.

He had a point. The tree was now bent slightly back, out of line with the orderly row of the rest of the trees. The Dubuques, I knew, did like to be orderly.

"You'll need a gigantic splint for the tree," Pantelli called down helpfully. "And don't forget to talk to the tree while you prop it back into place. Trees *hear*, you know."

Doubtless Pantelli meant well, but Mr. Dubuque only grew angrier. He spluttered out some words that Madge and I had always been strictly forbidden to use.

Meanwhile, the masked burglar was hobbling into the Dubuques' backyard.

"Him!" Mother, Madge and I shouted, pointing along the side of our house at the burglar.

"Her!" shouted Liesl, pointing at me.

In fairness, from where she stood, Liesl probably hadn't seen the burglar. But there was nothing fair in her expression. In Liesl's sharp white face, her dark eyes glittered with malicious pleasure.

What was worse, Talbot then laughed.

"I might have known," wailed Mr. Dubuque, glowering up at me.

"Don't be silly, Albert," said Mother, a rare impatient note in her voice. "Dinah isn't Hercules. She's not able to twist trees out of shape."

Trust Mother, in a crisis, to respond with a literary reference. Mother loved books—in fact, she was finishing her last course before getting her library science degree.

However, the reference was lost in the approaching wail of police sirens. The masked burglar hobbled out the Dubuques' back gate into the alley.

I glared at Talbot—and at Liesl, who, smirking at all the commotion, was pulling at her wedge.

# Chapter 4

*A simply smashing launch*

PULL ONLY IN CASE OF EMERGENCY.

I studied the sign over the glass-encased, red fire alarm on the *Empress Marie*'s deck. One of her decks, to be precise. There were eleven on the 91,000-ton ship that had initially reminded me of a fat white bar of soap. Some bar of soap. Steel, glass and marble a thousand feet long, with a beam (that's nautical for width at a ship's very widest part) of 105 feet wide.

"There won't be any emergency, small fry," Jack assured me, his gray eyes amused. "Not with Mr. Trotter around, running the *Empress* like a drill sergeant."

We'd already seen the program manager. He'd fluttered by us, patting his waxed mustache agitatedly and snapping out orders to every ship's steward he passed. Such as: "Make sure the Helpful Hints suggestion box is polished every day!"

"What if Julie's masked burglar follows her on board?" I demanded.

I leaned on the railing and surveyed the two thousand or so people sardined into Vancouver's cruise ship terminal below. Being a performer, I'd got to board early, bringing Mother and Madge with me. Like Jack, for this one week I was a member of the Happy Escapes Cruise Lines staff.

The regular passengers faced a longer wait, what with checking in their luggage and getting through U.S. customs. I could tell they were growing impatient; a lot of the faces below me were scrunched into grimaces.

But was the masked burglar anywhere among those faces? All I knew about him was that he was slight, about five nine—and had gooseberry-colored eyes.

And that he loathed brussels sprouts.

After showing up at our house, the police had found one witness, the next block over, who'd spotted a man in black hobbling into a battered Volkswagen van. The man had, the witness said, been chewing something—with his mouth pursed in utter distaste.

Okay, so his taste buds were normal even if his morals weren't, I thought. I scanned the crowd, admittedly a useless exercise since I couldn't see eye color from here.

"That and the sea air will soon put our masked trellis-breaker out of your mind," Mother was saying—not without a certain pleading note in her voice. She knew me too well.

I hadn't heard the first part of what she'd said. "*What* and the sea air?" I demanded.

Madge treated me to a sweet, sadistic smile. "Why, the swimming lessons Jack's going to give you, Di. He's signed you up. A private half-hour lesson every day of the cruise."

At long last passengers were being allowed up the gangway. I'd intended to scrutinize each of them for gooseberry eyes, but this horrifying pronouncement distracted me.

"WHAT? No way. You know I have a phobia about water." And I did. With my glasses off, everything was a frightening blur, the sides of the pool vanishing while the water engulfed me.

Mr. Trotter had bustled to the top of the gangway to greet passengers. "You'll love it here," he assured them. "At Happy Escapes we pride ourselves on the soothing quality of our vacation."

"Everyone should learn to swim, Ms. Dinah-mite," Jack was saying.

"We offer card games, afternoon movies..." Mr. Trotter went on.

"An important skill," Jack continued to me.

"Hot chocolate, massages..."

"Sadism," I corrected Jack, scowling.

Mr. Trotter nodded happily at the oncoming passengers. "Sadism...WHAT!?" He whipped round, mustache curls bobbing, to glare at me.

Jack grinned. "Sorry, Mr. T. Dinah was just complimenting me on my poolside manner. In her own jesting way, of course."

The program director narrowed his rather beady black eyes at the four of us. "No trouble," he said through gritted teeth. "Is that understood?"

Then he jabbed a forefinger close to Jack's freckled nose. "And NO HUMOR, young man."

"Right," said Jack.

Mr. Trotter reminded me of the producer of the play I'd been in last fall. He'd been humorless too. And he definitely hadn't liked me. I seemed to have trouble with authority figures.

A heavily perfumed and made-up woman in a mink coat stepped off the gangway. Mr. Trotter put on his most fawning smile, clapped his hands and oozed, "So sorry not to pay attention to you, Mrs. Figg. I was trying to deal with one of my performers. Sometimes they're not quite..." He tapped the side of his head and shrugged.

## "Preparing to sing?"

A man with shiny black hair tied into a ponytail was peering down at me. He wore faded green sweats and had wonderful, deep laugh lines around his eyes and mouth. He looked ready to start laughing now.

I realized my own mouth was still hanging open in response to Mr. Trotter's rudeness. What a horrid man! Now I wasn't sorry about eating his sandwich at all.

"You were people-watching, I bet," the man said. "I don't blame you. Look at that strange fellow."

At the bottom of the gangway, *Empress* officers were checking people's tickets. Just beyond the officers, a slight, fair-haired young man was glancing around impatiently. Waiting for someone, I guessed. He kept twitching around and bumping into people—"OW!" exclaimed a short, bald man, his head rammed by the young man's shoulder.

I didn't blame the bald man for being upset. His otherwise smooth dome now sported a red mark.

The young man twitched in our direction and happened to look up. He saw me and the black-haired man looking at him.

I stared—*really* stared—back.

The young man's eyes were gooseberry-colored.

He was the would-be thief, all right; he'd plainly recognized me. Whipping round, he charged into the cruise ship-terminal crowd, crashing into many more passengers.

"Clumsy guy," observed Jack.

"Yes!" I exclaimed. "Gooseberry-eyed and klutzy: that proves it. That's Julie's inept thief. Everything he touches, he damages."

Jack looked confused. Obviously he hadn't heard about the attempts to steal the Raven mask. (I *knew* Madge never talked about anything interesting to him.) He began sniffing the air. "Avast, me hearties! Is this another Dinah Galloway mystery I smell on the wind?"

"No," Madge told him coolly. "It's my Chanel No. 5. I put it on this morning thinking someone *might* appreciate it."

"Hey," said Jack, and beamed adoringly at her.

I rolled my eyes away from them—and met the amused blue ones of the man with the black ponytail. "Hi," I said in surprise. I'd forgotten about him.

"Hi," he smiled. He put out his hand. "I'm Evan Brander, your pianist for the cruise."

"Oh, wow," I said and shook his hand vigorously until it occurred to me that maybe you weren't supposed to do that to pianists. They probably had to be careful of their fingers. "Sorry," I said. "Next time I'll give you my special dead-fish handshake."

I put on my nicest smile. I really wanted to get along with my pianist this time. The last pianist I'd had, a large Scot named Graham, I'd completely alienated. Without meaning to, of course.

Mother blurted out to Evan, who was regarding me with surprise, "We're so pleased to meet you, Mr. Brander. I'm Suzanne Galloway, Dinah's mom. I'm afraid we must seem..." She hesitated, surveying me, Madge and Jack in confusion. "Well, you know what Tolstoy said. I mean, about happy families all being the same. Well, we Galloways are quite happy. But I've often wondered if Tolstoy didn't overlook happy families that were a bit odd... I can't imagine another family being the same as mine."

"*Mother.*" Madge was furious.

"Madge doesn't like being described as 'odd,'" Jack explained to Evan. "Hi, I'm Jack French. A devotee of the Galloway family, odd or not." He reached over to shake Evan's hand—much too hard, I thought critically. I'd have to speak to Jack about this later.

"It's obvious you guys have a lot of fun together," Evan said. Then, apologetically, to Mother, "Do you mind if I borrow Dinah for a while? I thought we might go over some tunes for tonight."

"A very sensible idea," Mother nodded—and I knew she was hoping work would distract me from my suspicions.

I took one last glance down at the terminal. I was able to spot Gooseberry Eyes because he was the only person trying to get out instead of in.

*Bash!* He tripped against an elderly woman, knocking her glasses off. She fell to her knees and began groping around blindly. Having often misplaced my own glasses, I understood what she was going through.

"Wow," observed Jack. "I've heard of smashing champagne glasses at a launch, but eyeglasses?"

Rather than stay to help, Gooseberry Eyes gave a panicky look back at the *Empress Marie*. He scanned the gangway and the deck. Briefly his gooseberry eyes met mine again.

Flinching, he bolted through the nearest door marked EXIT.

Which happened to lead into a stairwell. His legs flew up behind him and he went tumbling.

# Chapter 5

## A whale of an encounter

Julie joined Evan and me in the lounge where we were rehearsing. I told her about Gooseberry Eyes while Evan warmed up the songs from *Oliver!* that we'd be performing.

"Don't worry about the clumsy thief," Julie soothed. "Now that we've sailed, *I'm* not going to worry. Hey, get a load of that view!"

Vancouver was sliding by, and the blue-violet Coast Mountains; we were steaming into the Strait of Georgia to follow the rugged British Columbia coast north. The *Empress* would eventually build up to an average cruising speed of twenty-four knots.

Evan tinkled out a last few warm-up notes. "Ready?"

He and I were to perform from 5:00 to 7:00 every evening, with short breaks in between for him to rest his fingers and me my voice.

The lounge was more a place for people to have appetizers than meals. There were plenty of those in the main dining room, seating 1,200 at a time and open from 6:30 a.m. till after the midnight buffet. You could also order food to your stateroom round the clock.

And if all that wasn't enough, waiters roamed the decks with gleaming silver trays of nummy snacks. I'd tucked back several sweet biscuits piled with fluffy salmon pâté.

How appropriate that "Food, Glorious Food" was to be one of our songs! As I finished the last notes, I decided it should really be the *Empress Marie*'s theme song. Huh. Maybe I could make that joke during my performance. I'd seen old TV shows of my idol, Judy Garland, in concert, and she used to wisecrack between songs.

"Dinah, glorious Dinah," murmured Evan, tinkling out some random notes of a non-*Oliver!* song. "Where'd you get that voice, kiddo? It's a mixture of stardust and sweat."

"Uh…" I said. All I knew was that Mother referred to my voice as a godsend. The man she was seeing, Jon Horowitz, who'd been the director of the play I was in, said my voice made him think of the earthbound human heart expressing heavenly longings.

I thought both their opinions were daft. "All I do is sing," I said, shrugging.

"If people are born with talent, they should use it," Julie commented.

I hoped she wasn't going to get goopy about my voice too. But then I noticed her faraway expression.

She smiled apologetically. "I was thinking of myself. Of how the art dealer I told you about praised my work. Said it was so stark—so melancholy—and yet so beautiful."

"Great," I said politely, though sad stuff didn't really appeal to me. Madge had once shown me a picture of a painting called *War*, full of dead bodies. She'd enthused about how brilliant the painting was. Like, give me a break, Madge.

"Keep trying, and your talent will be appreciated," Evan advised Julie. He trilled some more notes up the keyboard—boy, that was a catchy tune. "One day you'll be discovered."

I thought of how I'd been "discovered." I was stuck in a broom closet and had to sing my way out. Mr. Wellman had heard me and signed me on as a client.

However, it was not a career strategy I could recommend for Julie. The broom closet had been dark and musty.

I was able to say, in all honesty, "Know what, Julie? Evan's right. Keep on with your painting. Look at my sister. She paints and sketches almost nonstop, even when you're talking to her."

"And what about you, Dinah?" Evan inquired. "Would you have kept singing if you'd never been discovered?"

"You betcha," I said promptly. "In the kitchen, on the street, wherever. When I was three, my dad brought me downstairs and plunked me in front of some dinner guests. He started playing the piano, and I started belting out. 'Frog, He Went A-Courtin'' I think it was, though exact wording wasn't my strength at the time."

I stopped to scowl away some tears that had been forming. I'd realized for a while now that, in a way, I was still singing for my dad — even though he was no longer around. He'd died a few years back in a car accident. His own fault, because he'd been drinking. As in, drinking a lot.

"Anyhow, if you gotta sing, you gotta sing," I mumbled.

"You're a true artist, Dinah," Julie told me in her soft voice. "And, unlike me, you have family who appreciate your talent. It's so unfair when a person doesn't." She gave my hand a squeeze and said she'd better go unpack.

She walked rather slowly and sadly across the velvety-carpeted lounge to the double doors, which were blue and imprinted with the Happy Escapes Cruise Lines logo of a fat white ship.

I thought, Julie sure broods about her stepsister a lot. Why does she bother?

I should've gone to unpack too — my Game Boy, my Deathstalkers comics, my CDs — but I was enjoying Evan's playing too much to leave.

"What is that tune?" I demanded.

"I don't know yet," said Evan. Idly, he tinkled some more of the refrain.

"You mean you wrote it? Wow!"

"Oh, I'm always writing songs." Evan gave me a rueful grin. "I love writing music—it's my second-favorite occupation, after being a dad."

"I bet you're a great dad," I said sincerely. "Did you bring your kids along?"

"My daughter's too young," Evan said with regret. "She'd need too much looking after. So my wife's at home taking care of her."

"You must miss them," I said sympathetically.

He started to tell me more about his family—but the double doors opened. Madge and Jack appeared.

Madge had a shopping bag with the words *Bathing Boutique* on it. With a sweet—read, sadistic—smile, she pulled from it a brand-new girl's bathing suit.

My size, not hers.

**"That's nice, Madge,"** I said, surveying the one-piece, emerald green suit with frilly black trim. "But are those really Jack's colors?"

I then tried to sprint between them, to escape. However, Jack's hand descended on my shoulder so that I ended up running on the spot and escaping nowhere. "As a friendly reminder, small fry, this was the deal you made with your mom. You could miss a week of school—if you agreed to take swimming lessons aboard the *Empress Marie*."

"I sort of remember that," I grudgingly admitted. I continued running on the spot, just in case he let go—

He didn't. "There was much pleading, I recall, especially in light of a certain social studies test you'd got back that day. Consisting of a map of Canada on which you were supposed to have labeled the major rivers, lakes and bays."

Jack lowered his freckled face to my level. His gray eyes were not amused. "A space alien, visiting Earth and seeing what you handed in, Ms. Galloway, would deduce that we Canadians hadn't got round to naming any of our bodies of water."

I ceased my running on the spot. I remembered that test very well. Pantelli and I had been busy trading Deathstalkers cards. "Fine," I sulked, grabbing the suit from Madge. "I'll meet you at the *Empress Marie*'s pool."

"In half an hour, small fry."

An *or else* hung in the air, as if it were washing on a clothesline. "I'm sorry I ever brought you two together," I told Jack crossly.

Because I had, last summer. Madge had been going out with a total dweeb at the time.

Jack must have remembered last summer too. He grinned. He never could stay stern for long. "No, you're not sorry you did," he said and kissed me on the forehead.

**It took us more** than half an hour, because the *Empress Marie* turned out to have three swimming pools, not one.

Madge and I kept asking directions from stewards bearing trays. And each time we did, I'd lift a nummy appetizer from the tray...

I started waddling instead of walking. "I might sink in water," I speculated, but Madge was too busy ooo-ing over the shops we passed, with designer this and designer that displayed in elegant little windows.

"Do you realize the *Empress Marie* has 14,000 square feet of shopping?" my sister enthused, in exactly the same awed tone other passengers at the railing were using to describe the orca whales they'd just spotted.

I waddled over to the railing to try and see for myself a gleaming black fin amid the slate-colored waves.

But Madge pulled me onward. "Jack's waiting," she scolded — after dawdling to ogle a Chanel purse.

"Mflgmfgtch," I retorted through the mouthful of prawns I'd just grabbed off a passing tray. Madge glanced at me oddly as I crunched the prawns. I didn't know what her problem was: I just happened to prefer them shell-on.

Word had spread about the orcas. People started cramming that particular deck. Among them, I saw the elderly woman whose glasses Gooseberry Eyes had knocked off. They were now back on her nose, though thickly masking-taped. With the force of the crowd, she was being bundled up against the railing.

I felt sorry for her. "That woman could use a life rope," I remarked to Madge.

Except that Madge was gone, lost in the scrunch of bodies. She'd probably moved on to that perfume boutique over there. But, being short, I couldn't see.

I began to wish I hadn't gobbled quite so much off the passing trays. Stuffed as I was, I sure couldn't move very quickly.

Forget orca whales. I was a beached one.

However, not for nothing were my friend Pantelli and I the champion belchers of Lord Bithersby Elementary. I summoned up my loudest one ever.

With distasteful looks, the people around me edged away. I darted over to the perfume boutique, positive Madge would be there, dreamily choosing between *eau de* this and *parfum de* that.

No Madge.

"Oh dear," moaned someone behind me. "I could use some smelling salts, if they have any."

It was the elderly woman with the masking-taped glasses. "So crowded," she murmured. "I have a phobia about crowds..."

In a rare tactful impulse, I stopped myself from demanding what, for goodness' sake, she was doing on a *cruise*. Instead I took hold of her arm and led her into the boutique.

"I need something strong," the woman told the sales clerk. "I feel so faint..."

The sales clerk, thin and pinch-faced, was busy craning out the boutique window for a glimpse. "That must've been thrilling! I wish *I* could get out to see a whale," she complained.

"I wish I could have a peaceful cruise," the elderly woman shuddered. She attempted to straighten her glasses, which the wad of masking tape was weighing down on one side. They immediately slipped into a diagonal slant again. "First I got crashed into, and now masses of people smother me."

Spying a nearby tester bottle, she began spraying its contents rather wildly around her. "That's better. Most soothing," she breathed.

I, too, was now doused with the perfume, called Sinful Satin. A sickly floral scent. *Stupid* Satin would be a better name for it, in my view. "Does anybody have a gas mask?" I demanded.

"Excuse me, madam." The clerk tried to tug the Sinful Satin away from the elderly woman, who, in her distress, was continuing to spray freely.

"Let's go outside, dear," the elderly woman suggested to me. "I'm afraid we've made a bad impression. I'm Lavinia O'Herlihy. Do you know what else I am?"

A bit weird, I answered her silently.


**But as we stepped** out on the deck, I already liked Lavinia. Behind her crooked glasses, her blue eyes had a definite twinkle.

"I'm a fan of yours," the old lady continued. "I saw you in *The Moonstone*. That's how I know who you are, Miss

Dinah Galloway. You were wonderful. What a voice! I went with several friends, and believe me, we all switched our hearing aids off. No need for 'em!"

"Thank you," I said and giggled. I'd never had a compliment put quite that way before. And Lavinia's timing was good, too, because I was still smarting over Talbot's and Liesl's insults. Break the sound barrier, indeed. Huh!

"I'm interested in finding out about the man who crashed into you," I said as Lavinia once again vainly tried to straighten her glasses. "I think he may be a thief. A would-be one, anyhow."

Lavinia stared at me, then let out a snort. "Dinah, all I know is that anyone who would shove old ladies down is slimy, cowardly, inconsiderate—"

"Dinah!" exclaimed Madge, breezing up to us. "Where'd you go? I thought I'd lost you. We've got a swimming lesson to get you to."

I was about to question Lavinia further about her Gooseberry Eyes experience when Madge suddenly gave a huge, and very disapproving, sniff.

"Di, what're you doing wearing Sinful Satin? It doesn't suit you at all."

# Chapter 6

*Not exactly in the swim of things*

I splashed about in the middle of the pool.

"I've conquered my fear of the water," I called to Jack. "Can I come out now?"

"The *wading pool* doesn't count, Ms. Galloway." With a crook of his thumb, Jack gestured to the main swimming pool, which stretched, it seemed to me, for ominous miles.

I trudged out of the wading pool and stood beside the main pool's shallow end. "Do you know how many people drown each year in mere inches of water?" I asked Jack. "I mean, have you seen the *stats*?"

"IN," ordered Jack.

That first lesson wasn't so bad. He held on to my waist while I kicked my feet and rotated my arms.

"Good. Relax, though," he instructed. "Remember what I've told you to do, but don't think about it, if you know what I mean."

At the moment of replying, my mouth was underwater. "Glub, glub," I said.

I lifted my face to expound on this, but Jack told me to keep practicing my crawl. After a while he exclaimed, "Hey, you're doing pretty well, Di. Let's see if you can swim on your own."

He let go of me—and I promptly sank.


**I stood on the end** of the diving board. At the blue bottom of the pool, an octopus-sized version of the white cruise ship logo shimmered at me.

Since I wasn't expected to dive in, I didn't feel nervous. Plus, my lesson with Jack being over, I had my glasses on again. Jack said that if I knew how to swim, blurry vision wouldn't matter—but I didn't believe him. He didn't understand what it was like.

Mr. Trotter was nearby, straightening the deck chairs into orderly rows. Noticing me, he glanced over at Jack, as if for help. But Jack was busy telling his first group of students the rules of the pool. These beginning swimmers were kindergarten age, which was why I'd refused to join the beginners' class. I mean, I would have been with *tinies*.

"I hope the staterooms are secure," I called to the program director. I was thinking of Julie Hébert and the mask she was keeping in her room.

Mr. Trotter creaked a last chair into place and glared at me. "Of *course* the staterooms are secure." He checked his watch. "I'm in rather a hurry, Miss Galloway, so I don't have time to waste on frivolity."

"Always walk slowly and carefully around the pool," Jack was telling the tinies, who were looking very chubby and cute in their life jackets.

I remembered what Mr. Wellman had told me about not creating trouble, but I couldn't help myself. "I'm not frivolous," I informed the program director. "I'm very businesslike. It's just that I'm concerned about things that might go missing."

Mr. Trotter's face had darkened to an unbecoming beet color. I shouldn't have bothered him. Memo to self: Always listen to your agent.

Jack told the tinies, though he was frowning in my direction, "No fooling around on the diving board *when you can't swim.*"

Suddenly, behind me, at the edge of the deep end: "Look who it is—the brussels sprouts queen!"

I whirled.

Talbot St. John! In swimming trunks, with a towel round his neck and a teasing grin around the soulful features Liesl found so appealing.

Second memo to self: Never whirl on a diving board.

My heels slid, meeting only air. I wobbled, flailing to regain my balance—

I fell backward.

As I hit the water, I could already see the huge splashes rising to smack squarely against Mr. Trotter...

"So now Talbot—a total twerp, by the way—has been banned from the indoor pool," I told Evan, who was tinkling out his as yet nameless tune in a warm-up for our performance.

Which was about to start. People were wandering in, settling at little round tables and eyeing the lists of appetizers and drinks on the two-sided, stand-up cards they found before them.

At the sight of the cards, I forgot my indignation at Talbot—for the moment. I thought, Yup, I'll try out my joke about "Food, Glorious Food" being the ideal theme song for the *Empress Marie*. Maybe I'll soon be known for my wit as much as my singing!

Mother and Madge came up to wish me luck. "That's a catchy tune," Mother complimented Evan. "You should try to sell it."

"Gotta think of some lyrics first," Evan replied, pleased. "Dah DAH dah dah DAH dah," he murmured along with the notes and then shook his head. "The SONG with no NAME yet. Nope, the words aren't coming to me."

"Paul McCartney went through the same thing," Mother reminded him. "For ages, the only title he could think of for 'Yesterday' was 'Scrambled Eggs'."

Evan laughed. "'Yesterday' was a definite improvement. Thanks for encouraging me, Suzanne. I'll keep trying."

"Dah DAH dah dah DAH dah," I sang along happily. "It's a great tune. It makes you jumpy, in a nice kind of way." I began to hop from one foot to the other. It was partly the tune and partly the rush of energy I always got when about to perform.

Madge winced. "Please don't do that, Dinah. I've already got a touch of seasickness."

"Ah, seasickness, the scourge of cruising," I nodded. "Were you paying attention at orientation, Madge? They said it gets way worse when we head out to open sea." I gave her a friendly elbowing. "Heave ho, get it? *Heave* ho." I hooted appreciatively at my wit.

"Madge and I will sit down now," Mother informed me. She led my sister, who'd grown rather pale, to their front-row table.

Evan chuckled. "I'm not sure this 'twerp,' as you call Talbot, realizes what he's in for, taking you on, Dinah."

"Jack really reamed him out for scaring me," I said in satisfaction. I giggled. "That was after Jack had plunged in to save me—dousing Mr. Trotter a second time. Oh well," I added philosophically. "I might not even see Talbot again on this cruise. I mean, there are two thousand passengers milling around."

Evan grew concerned, as grown-ups always do sooner or later in a conversation. (This is what makes talking to them for any length of time so trying.) "I'll do my best to watch out for him, Dinah. There's no reason your week on the *Empress* should be ruined by personality clashes."

I stared at him. "In my view, personality clashes tend to *enhance* an experience," I protested — but by then Evan was thrumming out the introductory notes to "Food, Glorious Food", and it was time for me to sing.

When the applause died down, I tried out my joke about "Food, Glorious Food" being the cruise theme song.

Silence. People paused in chomping on their appetizers to gaze at me bewilderedly. Only Jack, who'd slipped in late after his lesson with the tinies, grinned. Beside him, Mother had been too busy fussing over an increasingly sickly-looking Madge to hear.

"Huh!" I commented. "Guess I better stick to singing for a living."

Applause. *That* joke they all liked — go figure! I giggled and they clapped some more. I realized something: an audience and I get energy from each other.

Granted, that's after the initial terror of stepping out in front of them.

I started in on my mother's favorite song from *Oliver!* — "Who Will Buy?" A great belter-outer. I kept the beginning of the song shy and sad-sounding, though, the way Evan and I had rehearsed it. I became a wistful London Cockney girl, hoping against hope someone would buy her red roses.

I had a portable mike, so I strolled around between the tables as if I really did have a basket of roses to offer, just like in the play.

"Who will buy my sweet red roses?"

I sang the next verses louder, building up to the agonized part where the singer begs someone at least to notice what a beautiful morning it is. Maybe they'd buy *that* — but of course what she wants is what you can't buy: love.

When I finished, I saw that a bunch of elderly women were mopping at their eyes with blue napkins imprinted with fat white ship logos. "So lovely, dear," sobbed Lavinia O'Herlihy from the middle of the group. She raised her glasses so she could stuff the napkin against her streaming lids.

I covered the mike. "Hey, Lavinia, you got your glasses fixed!"

"There's an optician on board," sniffled Lavinia.

"On a cruise ship, there's everything you could possibly need," said another woman, and they all nodded.

Except for the oldest of them, who I saw now was actually a man. White-haired and spindly, he was hunched so far forward the tip of his nose was practically stirring the bowl of soup in front of him. "WHAT'S GOING ON?" he shouted peevishly. His tiny dark eyes blinked hard in the steam rising from the soup.

"IT'S ALL RIGHT, IRA." Lavinia patted the frail old man on one of his tweed-jacketed shoulders. "WE'LL FILL YOU IN LATER.

"Deaf as a post," she explained to me. "This is Ira Stone of Stone Construction. I've read about his financial empire in the newspapers. " And, winking, Lavinia rubbed her thumb and fingers together to signify that Ira had pots of money.

Wow. Lavinia was after Ira. Or after his pots of money, at any rate. And quite open about it. What a gal!

I guessed the song was wrong. You *could* buy love—the love of someone else for your money, that is.

Evan was playing the intro to my next song, "As Long As He Needs Me." Another belter-outer. A romantic one. It would certainly suit Lavinia's mood—too bad Ira wouldn't be able to hear it.

During one of the breaks, I went back to Lavinia's table. I wanted to ask her about Gooseberry Eyes. Could she give me a good description of him?

However, when I started to speak—

"STUFF AND NONSENSE!" shouted Ira. He'd been served another snack. This time the tip of his nose was almost touching a bowl of rice pudding.

"Later, dear," Lavinia told me, a little curtly. "Ira needs help with his food." Turning away, she picked up Ira's spoon, dipped it in the pudding and began to feed him.

At my next break I hung around Lavinia some more, but she ignored me. "Lavinia's determined to become the next Mrs. Ira Stone," one of the other ladies twinkled. "Must be your wonderful singing, Dinah. You're a regular Cupid."

Huh. I didn't know if I could agree with that. Granted, Cupid and I were both chubby. However, I was hardly into flying around naked and shooting arrows into people.

Julie Hébert slipped into the lounge when I was singing "Consider Yourself." Her face grew sad when I reached the line "Consider yourself part of the family." Doubtless she was thinking about her stepsister—oh well. Maybe if I blasted out the song, I could blast Elaine right out of her thoughts.

I planted my feet apart, tipped my head back, held the mike up and let the eardrum-splitting finale of the song rip. In my view, a good voice isn't something to be used sparingly, like the family silver.

"CONSIDER YOURSELF ONE OF U-U-U-U-U-S!"

Whoa. People were standing to applaud! On and on. Holy Toledo!

I turned and gestured for Evan to rise and get lots of applause too. It was inspiring to think that our performance had the power to make people happy.

Uh, not quite everyone.

Straight ahead of me, at the front-row table, Madge was throwing up into her purse.

# Chapter 7

*Lavinia, she went a-courtin'*

With careful planning I was able to fit four cheese blintzes on my plate. I made a second layer on top, of papaya wedges. Then, the crowning glory, a third layer of fat wedge fries.

"I wish Pantelli was here to see this," I told Jack. "He's a champion food stacker as well."

"I doubt Happy Escapes Cruise Lines could afford both of you," Jack replied.

From the 130-item buffet, he'd selected eggs Benedict, toast and strawberries. In other words, only one layer! I shook my head at him.

"So how's Madge?" Jack demanded as we joined Mother and Julie at a table. "Seasick or not, she has to appear sometime." He stole a wedge fry from my top layer.

Well, I'd put a stop to that. I emptied a large part of our table's ketchup bottle over the fries. I then gave him an evil, cunning smile.

"About Madge," Jack reminded me. He couldn't ask Mother, because she was busy chatting with Julie.

"Oh, right. Madge." I waved a wedge fry around airily; a splotch of ketchup flew off and landed on the otherwise snowy cloth of the next table. Luckily no one had sat down there yet. "Madge asked me to explain that she can't see you ever again," I informed him. "Sorry."

"What?!" Jack stared at me, half-amused, half-exasper-ated.

"Because you saw her barf." I tackled one of the cheese blintzes with my fork. Num: nice and runny. My next words were somewhat indistinct. "I don't get it either. Pantelli threw up on the school bus last year, and he wasn't embar-rassed." I swallowed the mouthful of blintz and continued enthusiastically, "His aim was incredible. Right out the window, *splat!*, on a pedestrian."

"DINAH." Mother had homed in, the way grown-ups always do when you're telling an especially fun anecdote. "I think you can spare us the details."

Shrugging, I speared a papaya slice and gestured grandly with it at Jack. "Anyhow, Madge is ultra-embarrassed. I mean, this is a girl who looks perfect at all times. You've now seen her at less than perfect. Therefore, your relationship with her is kaput. Finito! In ruins! But she did say she'd be considerate and set you up with a classmate of hers, so you wouldn't have to remain girlfriendless."

"Ah yes?" Jack's gray eyes narrowed. They had a gleam in them that gave me the feeling Madge wasn't going to be able to dismiss him *quite* so easily. "And who might this classmate be?"

"Dora Hidzwill."

"Isn't she the one with the, er, skin condition?"

I swallowed another nummy mouthful of cheese blintz and shook my fork at him. "I said Madge was being considerate. Not *kind*."

At that moment, Lavinia and her friends, supporting the frail, bent Ira, appeared at the buffet entrance. I waved to indicate the free table next to us.

Lavinia barked out words of encouragement to Ira until, with a little shove, she plopped him into the chair directly to my right.

"I'll get you a nice plate of food. Of soft food," Lavinia assured Ira. "I suspect those teeth aren't your own, duckie. Nothing to be ashamed of, mind!"

"That's Lavinia O'Herlihy," I murmured to Julie. "She's the one who saw your thief yesterday."

Then I pitched my voice over Ira's bent head to Lavinia: "Have you seen Gooseberry Eyes since yesterday?"

"Why, no, dear. I've been too busy with this cute fella here."

Ira's dark eyes fairly snapped at her in annoyance. "STUFF AND NONSENSE!" the old man shouted.

"Oh, Ira!" Lavinia exclaimed. "C'mon, ladies, we'd better shift him over a seat."

For Ira, hunched so far forward, had dunked the tip of his nose in the ketchup splotch.

**Shrieks interrupted our** buffet breakfast just as I was reaching for a slice of chocolate pecan pie.

"LOOK! *They're closing in on us!*"

This sounded interesting. Mother, Jack, Julie and I went out on deck.

People were leaning over the railing, but this time not to watch for orcas. On both sides of the *Empress Marie*, gray masses of rock crept closer, closer ...

Another scream. It was Lavinia. She'd scurried up beside me only to grow faint. "I have claustrophobia," she moaned. "Ohhh ..."

She swayed. Jack caught her on one side and I on the other. Julie raised her eyebrows at me. I knew what she was thinking about Lavinia. *Eccentric.*

"Lavinia, weren't you at orientation?" I demanded. I attend meetings of any sort—and ask tons of questions, as well as give helpful advice. At home, for instance, I never miss a Block Watch meeting. I'm just sorry that the neighbors are having fewer and fewer of them.

"This is the infamous Seymour Narrows," I explained to Lavinia. "It's kind of a pun, right? Everywhere you look, you *see more Narrows*. Why, we're practically getting scrunched by the rock. Notice how the mighty *Empress* has slowed down. We're crawling through the Narrows." I chuckled in enjoyment. "Will we make it?"

Lavinia let out a second, more plaintive moan. Weakly she scrabbled in her dress pocket, producing the Sinful Satin tester from the perfume boutique. "Must…revive…myself…" Seconds later we were all getting doused.

Boy, if Madge thought Sinful Satin wasn't *my* style, she oughtta smell it on Jack.

"What is that, a pesticide?" he choked.

I was too busy coughing to continue with my Seymour Narrows explanation. I'd intended to say that the Narrows used to be lethal as well as cramped. Ships kept crashing into huge Ripple Rock, smack in the middle of the passage. Finally, in the 1950s, the British Columbia government hired an engineer to blow it up. *Ka-boom!*

It's still tricky to get through. The tide builds to sixteen knots—translation, ultra-strong—so ships have to time their passage very carefully.

Lavinia cackled, "I was going to return this tester. Didn't mean to walk off with it! But," she showed it to us, "now it's empty!" And she tossed it into the Narrows.

"A gift to Neptune, the god of the sea," remarked Mother, literary as always.

"That stench is being sent to Neptune?" coughed Jack. "In that case, we're probably in for a few tidal waves."

"Wait! There are 126 buffet items left for me to try!" I protested as Jack and Mother forcibly led me away.

They had other plans for me. I'd thought it would be a lazy day, since the *Empress* wouldn't be putting into port until tomorrow: Juneau, our first stop.

Cruises, I soon learned, are packed with activities. Sure, there were lots of comfy-looking deck chairs where I could have stretched out with the latest Deathstalkers comic book—

"Don't even think about it," warned Mother, who'd noticed me eyeing the chairs. She unfolded the ship's daily newsletter, *Hundreds of Happy Events*, filled with lists of what was going on. *Is there an event we don't have that you'd like us to include?* the newsletter asked. *If so, pop your idea into our Helpful Hints suggestion box, just outside the Captain's cabin!*

Mother browsed the newsletter. "There's a bridge tournament, bingo, swing and ballroom dance classes, volleyball, yoga...I think I'll check out the yoga."

"Di and I will go for volleyball," said Jack, with irritating enthusiasm.

"We can play volleyball anywhere," I told him. "I mean, here we are, on an Alaska cruise! We should be taking in British Columbia's rugged scenery." I started reading aloud from the back of the newsletter. " 'Her dark forests jutting out to the edges of her craggy cliffs...' "

"Dinah, we're *fogged in*."

It was true. A mist had plumped itself over the ocean. A few optimists were leaning on the railing, binoculars propped on their noses to look for whales. But most passengers were either shopping or indulging in one of the hundreds of Happy Events.

"Volleyball it is," I sighed.


POW!

I serve a mean volleyball, if I do say so myself. It sailed high over the net, beyond the eagerly reaching fingers of the other team, to the back row.

Where Jack punched it back over. Dang. That was the problem with having a natural athlete in your opposition.

But, in the front row of our team, Julie was ready. She sprang at the ball and *slammed!* it down on the other side of the net. Somehow Julie had lengthened herself in mid-jump, the way our cat Wilfred did when stretching to catch a fly.

I was used to Wilfred behaving like a Slinky—but Julie! Housecleaning must keep Julie in great shape, I thought.

Julie's fashionably untidy hair fell over her forehead, threatening to block her view. I loaned her a hairclip, shaped like a sleeping cat, that Madge had made for me. With smiled thanks, Julie used it to shove her hair back.

Jack grew extra cunning, and slammed my next serve well out of Julie's reach. When it was my team's turn to serve again, I shifted to the front row, ending up beside Julie.

"Is the Raven safe?" I asked her.

Julie laughed and pinched my cheek. Exercise and being outside—and not brooding about her sister, I thought—were good for Julie. Her brown eyes were sparkling; her complexion, rosy.

She replied, "The mask is locked in a formidable steel safe in my stateroom. The Raven himself wouldn't be clever enough to get out of that."

Julie shot up, Slinky-like, to spike—*BONK!*—a fast, spinning ball Jack had punched over. Our side applauded.

I forgot about threats to the Raven. Jack whammed the ball over. It bounced neatly on the top of my head, soared up—

And would have landed on our side, a loss for us, except that Julie spiked it back.

Our cheers were interrupted, however. Somebody on the other team objected that my "head return" wasn't in the volleyball rulebook.

"What rulebook? Where?" said everyone else. We just wanted to play. But we all ended up in a huddle to argue about it. Julie and I rolled our eyes at each other.

I happened to roll mine in the direction of a set of stairs coming up from a stateroom level. Halfway up the stairs, staring open-mouthed, was Evan Brander.

**Maybe the concept** of a volleyball court was a new and startling one to my pianist.

I didn't think so. Evan was surprised to see someone. He was looking at—

Julie?

Turning, Evan hurried back down the stairs.

"Weird," I muttered.

"Exactly," said Jack, addressing the person who'd complained. "This isn't pro volleyball, buddy. It's for fun."

He proceeded to lecture everyone about how sports were meant to build teamwork and friendship. How that was way more important than the actual score.

Yup, Jack was a natural to be a teacher, all right.

Meanwhile, my natural curiosity was acting up. Who had Evan seen to make him bolt like that?

To me, curiosity is like a huge bowl of chocolate ice cream. You can't resist it—especially if no one is noticing how much you indulge.

I slipped out of the huddle of arguing volleyball players. An advantage to being short was that I was beneath their line of vision.

I plunged down the stairs after Evan.

# Chapter 8
*Talk about your bad-hair days*

When I reached the bottom of the stairs, Evan was whisking around a corner. Whatever he was up to, he was in a tremendous hurry about it.

"Loved your show last night," a deep voice rumbled behind me. It was a handsome, grinning steward, wheeling along a trolley of trays and dishes that he'd been picking up outside people's doors.

Evan looked around. He was beside the fourth door down.

"Thanks," I told the steward and gave Evan my bared-teeth phony smile.

"What are you doing here, Dinah?" Evan asked—with a tinge of impatience.

"I...uh..." Panicky memo to self: Have excuses ready *before* these awkward moments occur. I brightened. "I thought we could work on some lyrics for your song. For dah DAH dah dah DAH dah."

"Oh." Evan seemed to thaw. "That's nice, Dinah. Not right now, though." He swiveled away from the door and walked off.

Why hadn't he gone into his room? I wondered. He'd been about to twist the knob.

Weirder and weirder.


**"They're still arguing,"** Julie greeted me, with a nod toward the huddle of players.

She noticed my expression. "Is something wrong, Di?"

I told her about Evan. "I had problems with my last pianist," I mourned. "My fault, I admit it. This time I really wanted things to be different."

Julie was gaping at me. "Did you say four rooms down? That's *my* room!"

I gaped at her in return. One of the ever-present stewards glided by with a tray. Assuming our mouths were open in readiness for food, he held out the tray.

For once my appetite failed me. "So Evan was skulking outside *your* room," I said faintly.

"Preparing to pick the lock, you think?" Julie asked. She

clutched her spiky hair. "This is too melodramatic, Dinah. Can't be true!"

Nevertheless, like a couple of anxious moms, we went down to check on the Raven. "I won't breathe easy until tomorrow's over," Julie confessed, unlocking her stateroom door.

A fat, squat gray safe sat against the wall. "Want to see the Raven again?" Julie invited. "After all, he'll soon be at the Juneau Heritage Gallery, secured behind thick, unbreakable glass rigged with all kinds of alarms."

A moment later, peeling away bubble wrap, Julie revealed the Raven. Over his red-rimmed beak, his sharp black eyes were bright with mirth, as if at his own cleverness. I couldn't help grinning back at him.

Julie noticed and nodded in understanding. "As with any art, masks never stop giving pleasure to the beholder," she said. "In fact, masks are part of a giving *ceremony*, if you will: the potlatch. That's a meeting of the tribal chiefs and other high-ranking members—but they're also feasts for everyone. Gifts abound. Dances, masks, songs and stories that celebrate the tribe, giving everyone a sense of belonging," Julie finished, rather wistfully.

She wrapped the Raven up again. "I'm afraid that's where my relationship with Elaine is flawed. She never accepts that I have talent at painting. To her, there's room for only one Hébert sister to be famous."

Dang it, Julie was off on *that* again. I was getting awfully tired of hearing about Elaine.

"And I do love art," Julie continued. "How about you, Dinah? Who's your favorite artist?"

I considered this. "Adams."

"Ansel?"

"Scott."

Julie smiled. "Perhaps you'd like to see one of my paintings before you go." After locking up the Raven, she lifted a placemat-sized canvas off the top of her night table.

I gasped. From the canvas, a madwoman leered out at me! Her eyes blazed. Her lips stretched way back from her gums. Her teeth loomed, huge, sharp and menacing, like knives.

Julie patted the canvas proudly. "I still have to do some work on it. Can't wait to show it to that dealer who was so interested in my work." She pointed to the lower right-hand corner. " '*Medusa*, by Julie Hébert.' Do you like it?"

I gulped. Mother had told me fibs were okay, even desirable, to avoid offending people. "I—I, " I began. The problem is, I find it unnatural to be anything except blunt.

"You've done interesting things with her hair," I got out finally.

Which was true. Julie had formed her subject's black locks of hair into snakes.

**When I told Madge** about it the next day, she shuddered. "Medusa was a character in Greek mythology. Snakes billowed out of her head, and everyone who made eye contact with her turned to stone."

"I guess that wrecked any chance of her getting beauty salon appointments," I huffed and puffed.

Along with a lot of other *Empress Marie* passengers, we'd taken the thirteen-mile bus trip from Juneau to the massive Mendenhall Glacier. Madge, however, had insisted on our leaving the rest of the group at the Visitors' Center to hike up the West Glacier Trail for a better view. Like Jack, Madge had an annoying athletic streak.

Jack would be taking a later bus to the glacier, when he got a break from work. Mother and Julie would be coming with him. First, though, they were escorting the Raven to the Juneau Heritage Gallery.

Madge was still shunning Jack, though I didn't see how she could keep on with it. I mean, what was one barfing episode between sweethearts?

At the moment, Madge was thinking about Julie Hébert's painting. "Too bad she doesn't paint happier mythic characters. Like Persephone, who signifies spring. Or Aphrodite, the goddess of love and beauty."

"Weird," I agreed, puffing.

"Dinah, please stop saying 'weird' so much. It's annoying."

After a while we flopped down in a meadow shimmering with color. Madge figured out the plant names from the wildflower guidebook she'd brought. The clusters of tiny white flowers were Indian rhubarb; the magenta sprays of blossom were shooting stars; and we already knew the lupines, exactly the brilliant blue shade of Madge's eyes.

Lucky Madge. I had ordinary old hazel eyes, a jumble of green, gray and brown that suggested nature hadn't been able to make up its mind about me.

On the other hand, the jumble of colors sort of reflected my personality. I did tend to barge off in all directions at once.

As I sat feeling, as usual, dissatisfied with my appearance, Madge astounded me by saying: "You're getting to be quite attractive, Dinah. That intensity, that fierceness, you've always had in your expression—in a bizarre, unexpected way, it's turning into prettiness."

Me, pretty? We'd climbed high; maybe the thin air was affecting my sister's brain.

Madge had her sketchbook out and was drawing the flowers around us. She'd note "magenta" or "royal blue," depending what flower she was doing, for water-coloring in later.

I was content just to gaze at the Mendenhall Glacier. Twelve miles long, one-and-a-half miles wide, it sits in the middle of Mendenhall Lake like a humongous blueberry Popsicle. Madge had been right to bring us up the trail. The glacier was brighter and clearer from here.

Ditto the 5,900 emerald peaks of the Mendenhall Towers, each with snow perched on top, trickling down here and there like a melting scoop of vanilla ice cream.

I tended to think of things in terms of food. Madge, however, was murmuring that the glacier resembled an aquamarine ring Dad had once given Mother.

A romantic gesture—except that Mother had to pay for the ring when the bill came in. Dad was off on one of his drinking binges. With Dad, the fun was offset by the frustrating. Which made the memories of him a teeter-totter. I would recall his encouragement about my singing—and then remember his binges.

I knew Madge was also thinking of how that particular romantic gesture had ended, because she gave a slight frown and immediately replaced it with a determined cheery smile. "Shall we eat?" Her long, slim fingers unclasped the wicker latches of the picnic basket the *Empress*'s chef had packed for us.

Madge had carried the basket up in her knapsack. I saw that another item she'd brought was binoculars. Reaching for these, I lay down on my stomach and trained them on the Mendenhall Glacier Visitors' Center. I wanted to see if Mother and Julie had arrived yet.

"There's Ira," I exclaimed, swirling the lenses into better focus. "He's hobbling off a tour bus, along with the doting Lavinia. Guess the bus we took was too early for them. STUFF AND NONSENSE!" I shouted. I found Ira amusing.

He couldn't hear me, of course, but a couple of mountain goats did. They were grazing in some clover, across the meadow from Madge and me. The goats glanced up, beards wagging as they chewed, and regarded me with scorn.

"STUFF AND NONSENSE!" I shouted again.

"*Please*, Dinah," begged Madge. "What have my ear-drums ever done to you?"

"There's Mother getting off the bus. And Jack! Wait—where's Julie? I thought she and Mother were both coming...Nope, Julie's not there. Weird."

"Dinah, PLEASE stop saying 'weird.' "

# Chapter 9

## A chilling experience

I spent the next minutes eating my favorite banana-honey-peanut-butter sandwich and watching Jack through the binoculars. Somebody had pointed him up the trail after us.

"He's sprinting all the way up," I informed Madge. "Can you believe it? *Sprinting!*"

Madge was looking annoyed and pleased at the same time. "There's no need to report on him, Dinah. This isn't ABC's *Wide World of Sports*."

When I'd finished my sandwich, I started bellowing "STUFF AND NONSENSE!" at Jack. It was a scientific experiment, you might say. To find out how far up the trail Jack would have to be before he heard me. "STUFF AND NONSENSE!" Yup, I was a regular Albert Einstein.

"DINAH!"

I lowered the binoculars. Madge was standing and glowering.

Then, to my amazement, her face crumpled and she burst into tears. By the time Jack reached us, I was trying to explain, "But, Madge, this is *science* ... "

Jack gathered her in his arms for a bear hug. After all that sprinting, he was only slightly out of breath. That wasn't athletic, in my view. It was unnatural.

Jack noticed my disapproving frown and winked at me. "So tell me," he murmured to Madge, "is it my personality that upsets you? Or should I just be switching deodorants?"

Madge giggled through her tears. That was the great thing about Jack. Being beautiful, my sister had always been fussed over by everyone. Spoiled, really. But Jack laughed at her instead of fussing.

With a shaky breath, Madge told him, "It's—well, sometimes having a younger sister is so *stressful*."

"WHAT?" I couldn't believe the unfairness of this. "Madge, you got on an emotional teeter-totter just now because of Dad, not me! You won't admit to thinking about Dad—it'd make things less than perfect, wouldn't it?"

Madge wouldn't look at me. Jack, however, was glancing back and forth from one to the other of us with the beginnings of understanding in his gray eyes.

"It's the Mendenhall Glacier's fault," I finished dramatically. "That's what started it all."

"Ri-ight," said Jack. Then, unexpectedly, "You're a sensitive kid, Dinah. I bet that's part of what reaches people when you sing. It's not just the voice."

Me, sensitive? That was the second shocking observation made about me within the hour. Beneath my annoyance at Madge, I felt the faint stirrings of pleasure.

"All right," said Madge, dabbing at her eyes with one of the blue-imprinted-with-white-ship napkins from the picnic basket. "I will acknowledge that my sister is stressful *and* sensitive."

She fished a brownie out of the basket and handed it to me. A peace offering. We gave each other tight, suspicious smiles and narrow-eyed frowns; it was what we did when making up. All in good humor—sort of. It's a sister thing, difficult for outsiders to understand.

"You should have some of this lunch with us," Madge told Jack, who was indeed looking bemused. "The chef packed enough for ten people. Or at least for Dinah and two friends."

"Can't, my one-and-only." Growing somber, Jack picked up the basket. "We should head back down to your mom. She's been through a bad shock."

With his free hand he pulled me close for my turn at a bear hug. Then he explained: "Your mother and Julie delivered the Raven by cab to the Juneau Heritage Gallery. Or tried to. When they stepped out of the cab, a young man in a black balaclava and ski suit rushed Julie. He grabbed the box and peeled down the street, out of sight."

"You mean—the Raven's gone?" I squeaked.

"Gone with the brisk Alaska wind. To use your favorite word, young Di, there's something even weirder. Your mom caught a glimpse of the guy's eyes as he was wrestling the package away from Julie.

"*His eyes were gooseberry-colored.*"

**You could definitely** call Jack's news a cliffhanger. We were near a cliff and my mouth was hanging open.

Jack didn't have a lot to add. Julie was giving a statement at the police station. The Juneau Heritage Gallery had announced that its famed Raven mask would not be returning soon, maybe ever.

I raced ahead of Jack and Madge down the trail. After all, it was I who'd had the original sightings of Gooseberry Eyes, off our balcony at home, and then at the Vancouver cruise ship terminal. It was my duty to tell the police about that.

Then there was Lavinia. She'd sighted Gooseberry Eyes at the terminal too—if only she'd stop wooing Ira long enough to tell the police!

No doubt about it. I had work to do.

**In zooming past** Jack and my sister, I'd scooped another sandwich out of the picnic basket. I chomped into it as I ran. Ew, cucumber and cream cheese. Cream cheese *lite*, no doubt. This would be the sandwich Madge had ordered.

At a bend in the trail I almost bumped into a group of *Empress Marie* passengers. In the lead, whistling, was—Talbot St. John.

The tune he'd been whistling died away at the sight of me. He ducked his face, as if trying to hide beneath the long, dark forelock Liesl and the other girls were mad over. "Hi, Dinah," Talbot said uncomfortably. "Listen, I'm sorry about the pool incident. I didn't mean to—"

"What pool incident, Talbot?" asked a sharp-faced woman behind him. In starched khakis, she had one of those pageboy hairdos so stiffly sprayed you feel you could break a sprig off and use it for firewood.

So that was Talbot's mom! No wonder he had such a scornful attitude; he must've got it from her.

I almost felt a twinge of understanding. Then I remembered how scornful he'd been about *me*. I turned my back on him. To show how gnat-like and insignificant his presence was, I busied myself training the binoculars on the Visitors' Center.

There was Mother. Closer now, I could make out the anxiety on her face. Hard to enjoy a view, even one as spectacular as the Mendenhall Glacier, when you'd just had a rare piece of art whisked out from under your nose.

There was stooped old Ira, being fussed over by Lavinia. She was trying to give him a steaming cup of something, hot chocolate maybe. He was swatting it away.

And Evan—he'd arrived by that later bus too. Evan looked just as anxious as Mother. Kept glancing up the trail as if afraid the abominable snowman was about to descend. What was his problem?

I heard Madge's and Jack's voices coming up behind me. Well, time to gallop ahead of them. I knew, I just *knew*, they were talking about their relationship. Teens did that. They went on for hours, all very solemnly, with vows and promises galore. Bo-o-r-ring.

I caught a scrap of their conversation. Jack was saying, "Love doesn't mean one or the other of us, or both of us, for that matter, has to be perfect."

YECH! I galloped. Soon I'd be at the bottom and could question Mother about Gooseberry Eyes — preferably over one of those cups of hot chocolate Lavinia had been trying to press on Ira.

**I met a second group** of passengers climbing the trail. There were so many of them I dodged into a tiny woods beside the lake. At this point the trail had almost wound to its base. If I'd sat down at the edge of the woods, my feet would have just about touched water.

This being a glacial lake, I decided to give that idea a pass. Instead, feet crunching on the dry pine needles beneath the trees, I hoisted the binoculars for another look round. There was a cormorant! Perched on a rock, the slim black bird bowed formally to me. I bowed back.

Of course he wasn't really bowing. He was watching for fish. *Plop!* His long neck plunged into the clear blue water. He lifted his head up again: a shiny silver trout was squirming in his long beak.

Only for a second, though. *Gulp!* Then he started bowing again.

I lifted the binoculars to focus on the Visitors' Center. Mother still wore her anxious expression. To cheer her up, I waved. "C'mon, Mother, notice me!"

As a result, I didn't really notice the people around her. Not at first. They would just be the same ones as before, right?

Hold on. I stopped waving. That was funny. They weren't quite the same. There was one difference. I refocused the lenses. Huh! I was right.

I was just pursing my lips to form my favorite word, *weird*, when it happened.

I was shoved roughly from behind and sent hurtling into Mendenhall Lake.

**Let's be more** precise about that.

Into *ice-cold, deep* Mendenhall Lake.

Forget the principle of flotation. I'd been pushed so hard I just sank. No cormorant, I. I went into the blue and then black depths, where all of me froze but my brain. Then, after I briefly, longingly, pictured Mother, Madge, Jack and Wilfred the cat, my brain numbed, too.

Except for a single, almost calm thought: The image of my loved ones breezed by awfully fast just now. Is that all there is?

*Is that all there is?* That was a song. My dad had played it a lot. Peggy Lee sang it. Dad had really liked Peggy Lee.

Numbed, I was growing comfortable. Didn't feel like moving at all. *Dad*... I could see him now. My dad had crisp black curly hair and black eyes so bright and full of life they practically gave off electricity. "Hey, Dinah," he'd say, starting up a CD. "See if you can sing this one."

*Dad?*

I don't know if I tried to call out to him. Ever after I *thought* I did. More likely—at least, this is what everyone said—water filled my lungs, and it was then that I started coughing and spewing out bubbles. And thrashing around in an effort to punch through that deep, blue-black cold.

Anyhow, I'd always believe that the thought of Dad forced me to the surface again.

Something grabbed me by an armpit. Something sharp. Must be the cormorant's beak. The beak dragged me up, up, out of the water.

After several huge wrenching coughs, I could breathe again. I gasped, "Did you run out of fish?"

"Trust Dinah to be thinking about food," said a familiar, rather shaky voice next to me.

I opened my eyes—they'd been squeezed shut. I was sitting on the pine needle floor. Madge was kneeling beside me, her face pale, frightened and tender at the same time.

Jack was on the other side of me. He had me gripped in another bear hug, as if he feared I might get away from him.

He was sopping wet. *He'd* been the cormorant.

"We're going to revise our swimming lesson plans," Jack informed me. His voice was unsteady too. "Since you seem unable to be around water without falling into it, I'm first going to teach you how to tread water. That way, next time, you can keep your head up while waiting for me to fish you out."

I could see how my impromptu plunges would get to be tiresome for Jack. I tried to apologize, but my teeth were chattering too badly.

"C'mon," said Jack, hoisting me. "Let's take our shivering bones down to the Visitors' Center. Maybe they have some towels."

"Paper towels, for sure, in the public washrooms." Madge allowed herself the ghost of a smile. "You can cover yourselves with them and pretend to be mummies."

They each took one of my hands and we hurried down the path. "I'm not letting this kid near a *glass* of water without supervision," Jack informed Madge.

I wanted to speak, to tell them that I was sorry. That it hadn't been my fault: someone had shoved me.

But what finally chattered out from between my teeth was: "I saw Dad."

# Chapter 10

## *A memory in the deep freeze*

They didn't believe me.

They also didn't believe that I'd be able to do a show in the evening. On that point, anyway, I was able to prove them wrong. I belted out just the same as always. Maybe more so, because I remembered how numbing those dark depths had been and how I'd almost given up and stayed there.

Nope, I wanted to live, and to live was to sing. In fact, I blasted out "Who Will Buy?" so loudly that people strolling by on the deck heard and crowded in to listen.

Later I planned to sing it again, maybe not *quite* so loudly, for Madge. Now that we were ocean-bound again, she was swaddled in comforters in our stateroom, suffering a fresh bout of seasickness.

"You're certainly a big draw," Mr. Trotter admitted after the show. He mopped delicately at his mustache curls with a blue-and-white napkin to remove any hors d'oeuvres crumbs. "If only you were, well, quieter in other respects."

I knew he was referring to what had happened at Mendenhall Lake. It was the talk of the ship.

Evan was tinkling out *dah DAH dah dah DAH dah*; he glanced up and smiled wryly. "I hardly think Dinah *chose* to be shoved in the lake, Mr. Trotter."

The program director's apple-like cheeks grew mottled. He didn't like being contradicted, especially by a lowly staffer.

Then he saw Julie, cute in a leopard print mini-dress and black fishnet stockings, and his expression became fond and beaming. He oozed out some compliment, but she ignored him.

"Who do you think pushed you, Dinah?" she asked, looking frightened. "Was it Gooseberry Eyes?"

"I don't know," I said unhappily. That particular whodunit had been bothering me all day. Or at least since a whole crowd of anxious fellow *Empress* passengers had pressed hot chocolates on me, and the intense sugar hit had revived my numb brain.

Evan kept playing. I fit the words in my mind to his tune: Who WAS it who PUSHED me? "I just didn't see," I admitted.

"Why would Gooseberry Eyes, having stolen the mask, then head over to Mendenhall Lake for a trail hike?" Mother wondered to Julie. "It doesn't make sense. Wouldn't he want to get as far away as possible, as fast as possible?"

"You'd think so," said Julie, clearly troubled.

"You'd *bet* so," I interrupted. "Gooseberry Eyes wants to sell the mask to some unscrup—unscrup —"

"Unscrupulous," Julie filled in, with a wan smile.

"Unscrupulous art collector," I finished. Mother often lectured me about interrupting, but it was hard not to.

Julie sighed. "Yes, our gooseberry-eyed thief must be long gone."

She frowned at Mr. Trotter, who'd been smiling admiringly at her. Embarrassed, the program director backed up—to bump into Jack. "You. *French*," Mr. Trotter blurted out. "Can't you watch where you're going?"

"It's evidently more in my interest to watch where *you're* going," Jack returned, nursing the foot Mr. Trotter had stepped on.

Jack had a lazy way of speaking, especially when delivering insults, so that people were left puzzling whether or not to feel offended.

*Dah DAH dah dah DAH dah*, played Evan, hiding a smile.

"I trust you're not being humorous again," Mr. Trotter snapped at Jack.

"Sorry," said Jack. "Dinah, did you see anyone on the trail before you went into those woods?"

"Just a bunch of people hiking up," I said. "*Empress Marie* people."

Evan shook his head over the notes he was playing. "And among them, possibly, a gooseberry-eyed outsider."

Mother shuddered. I would've shuddered too, except that I was hot and sweaty from singing. Besides, one face from the bunch of hikers had detached itself to hover, like a question mark, in my mind. A long, oval question mark with a black lock of hair tumbling over it. Talbot St. John.

Talbot had been among the hikers—and we didn't like each other. To him, I had about the status of the dirt underfoot on the West Glacier Trail.

Was scorn enough of a motive for him to push me into Mendenhall Lake? Talbot wasn't stupid. He was acing his grade seven science tests at Lord Bithersby (yet another reason to dislike him). He had to know that near-freezing water wasn't the healthiest thing to immerse a classmate in.

Sure, a bright guy like Talbot would know that.

But would it matter to him?

Mother bent down and whispered to me. "Dinah, you're scowling yourself into a little gnarled walnut. Is there something you want to tell me?"

"Um," I said. I couldn't bring myself to say what I'd been thinking. Twerpy or not, Talbot was a fellow Lord Bithersby-ite. Besides, I had no proof.

Mother took hold of my hand. Rather tearfully, she told the others, "Dinah—shy and reluctant to speak! This girl is *ill*. I knew it. One can't be tossed into glacial waters without some side effects. I'd better get her into a warm bed right away. Oh dear, I don't want her going the way of Ophelia..."

Oh no. The inevitable literary reference. I had no idea who Ophelia was, except that she must be of the drowned-rat variety. "Mother," I protested.

"Now, now, what's this?" a jolly voice demanded.

It was Captain Heidgarten. As in, the ship's captain. Broad-shouldered, in a starched white uniform brimming with gold buttons, he towered over the rest of us, even Jack, who was no slouch. Captain Heidgarten's blue eyes twinkled at us out of his brown-bearded, sunburned face. "I've been intending to pay my compliments to you, Dinah, on your singing abilities. I had the pleasure of seeing you in *The Moonstone* last fall and am looking forward to attending one of your performances aboard the *Empress*. But now I see I have to offer my congratulations to you as well. Anyone who survives the brutal clutches of the waters of Mendenhall is remarkable indeed.

"And congratulations to you, too, young man," the Captain said to Jack and shook his hand. "Everyone's telling me what a hero you were today. When we return to Vancouver, I intend to recommend you for a Royal Lifesaving Medal."

"Aw, no," mumbled Jack, blushing to the roots of his sandy hair.

The Captain clapped him on the back. "Be assured, there's a job for you on our Happy Escapes fleet whenever you want it."

"No!" choked Mr. Trotter. "That is," he coughed, as the Captain turned an inquiring gaze on him, "no doubt about it."

Captain Heidgarten smiled at me again. "So, my dear. I wanted to invite you and your family to dine with me this evening. Afterwards, I thought we might take in a show together. Hans and Roman, the famous magicians, are performing one of their now-you-see-it, now-you-don't extravaganzas. But it all depends on whether you've recovered."

Hans and Roman! I'd seen them on TV. Wouldn't miss out on this evening for anything. "That'd be great," I exclaimed. "Don't worry, that brief dip in the lake was ..." I shrugged to indicate how laughably insignificant my near-drowning had been. "Nope, I feel just fine."

And then I fainted.

**Forget Hans and Roman.** I had my own magic act: now you see Dinah, now you don't.

I tried to say this out loud. After all, I was dining with the ship's captain, so I should come equipped with wisecracks. Everyone at the table — Captain Heidgarten, Mother, Jack, Julie, Evan — stared at me expectantly.

"What was that, Dinah?" Madge asked.

I tried again. " ... You ... see ... Dinah ... "

"Of course I see you," Madge returned, sounding irritable. "These staterooms are small. It'd be hard to miss a red-headed lump in the bedclothes."

The faces and the dinner table evaporated. Dang, and there'd been grilled potato wedges, along with cheddar cheese-sprinkled sour cream to dip them in. I'd been about to reach for a particularly fat wedge...

I forced my sleepy eyelids partway open. I was in bed, all right. Those blurry surroundings would be our stateroom. That blurry auburn-haired girl over there on the chair would be my sister Madge.

"Why aren't you at dinner with the Captain?" I mumbled.

"Why do you think?" Madge asked bitterly. She staggered into the bathroom. Retching noises echoed back to me.

My eyelids were pretty heavy, so I let them fall again. Mother was right. The icy lake had taken a lot out of me. Like a few dozen degrees of body temperature, for starters. Mothers were always right, weren't they?

... Couldn't ever tell them that, though...

... There'd... be... no... standing... them...

Dozing off, I remembered how, from the tiny woods, I'd spotted Mother through the binoculars. How anxious and motherly she'd looked.

Then had come the shove...

I jolted awake again. Wait a minute. From the woods, yes, I'd been watching Mother through the binoculars. But I'd been watching the people around her, too.

Now I remembered. Something had been wrong with the scene I'd—pardon the pun—seen.

What was the something?

It was no use. My plunge into Mendenhall Lake had frozen my memory.

# Chapter 11
*Dinah's doom-and-groom attitude*

"Jack, you should go back upstairs and enjoy Hans and Herman."

"Hans and Roman, Madge. Anyhow, I needed a break. How many rabbits do I need to see pulled out of hats? Besides, all that fur was making my allergies act up."

"Jack, you don't *have* allergies. Now, I want you to leave before I get seasick again, or that really will be it for us. I mean it."

Their voices woke me. I'd been having one of those cool dreams about flying. The Lord Bithersby playground had been far below. Liesl Dubuque had gaped up at me enviously while tugging on that back wedge of hair she was so eager to grow.

By squinting I could just bring Madge and Jack into view. He'd pulled up the other of the two chairs in our stateroom and was sitting beside her. I guessed they'd reached in impasse in their discussion, because they were just looking at each other now. Even though Madge was annoyed, it was one of those mutual gazes neither of them seemed to want to break.

Teen love. YECH.

"Uh-oh," Madge said in alarm. "I knew this would happen—"

Jack grabbed the fat-white-ship-on-blue-background ice bucket off the desk and held it under her chin.

*BLEEEUUUCKK.*

Madge covered her face with her hands. Not because she was suffering. I mean, she'd been heaving for two days straight, so she had to be used to it. Nope, it was because she was humiliated.

Wide-awake now—who wouldn't be, after that *BLEEEUUUCKK*—I was about to assure my sister that she vomited with admirable flair.

But then Jack murmured to her, "Don't you know that I love you when you're imperfect as well as perfect? Maybe more so. It's human beings that people love, not goddesses."

Madge peeked through her fingers. The human side of

her was peeking, I thought suddenly. Checking to see if it was all right to venture out.

"Dinah's right about me," she said, her voice muffled by her hands. "Since we lost Dad, I've kept trying to smooth everything over. To keep appearances—*my* appearance included—perfect. I've polished the surface of my life again and again so the rough memories underneath wouldn't show."

She removed her hands and smiled, her face teary, splotchy and very un-Madge-ly. "I've been such a tidy, well-ordered person," she said.

Another one of those unbreakable gazes. Then, "You could try being messy and disordered sometimes," Jack suggested.

"I *will* try," Madge said. She grimaced. "If I could just stop throwing up. That's a little too messy and disordered."

Jack laughed. He went into the bathroom to empty the ice bucket in the toilet and rinse it out under the faucet. "Granted, we might not opt for a cruise on our honeymoon."

Honeymoon! I thought. HONEYMOON???

In a rare discreet impulse, I'd been staying quiet all this while. But with Jack talking about marriage—c'mon, I fumed. This was supposed to be *teen* love.

Okay, so Jack was *nine*teen. I didn't care. He still qualified. Marriage was out.

See, Mother, Madge, Wilfred the cat and I were, well, we were a unit. A foursome. It'd been the four of us together against the world since Dad died.

Okay, so not against the *world*, exactly. More like against the rough memories Madge had been describing. We'd been a foursome for ages in our house on Wisteria Street on Vancouver's Grandview hill. Madge couldn't leave, not yet. It'd be like detaching one of the walls of the house.

I was about to sit up and blurt out a series of indignant objections when Madge spoke.

"Honeymoon?!" she exclaimed.

That's it, Madge, I thought with satisfaction. Really let him have it.

"Honeymoon," she repeated softly, in a very un-let-him-have-it voice.

Jack sat down beside her again. "Is it wrong to talk about marriage?" he asked gently. "It doesn't feel wrong to me. But if you're uncomfortable, I can yearn in silence for a few more months. Years, if you prefer. Decades, I might utter a few peeps of protest at."

"Well..." Madge sounded uncertain. To my dismay, however, not horrified. "Right now I'm only seventeen."

"Juliet was fourteen."

Juliet, I thought grimly. As in *Romeo and*, no doubt. Great. Ideas about marriage weren't bad enough. Now Jack had to copy Mother and get into literary references.

I re-squinted at them over the covers. Yet another of those unbearable gazes was going on between them. Madge was looking pink and pleased; Jack, tender.

I HATE tender.

I sat up so fast the covers flew off me in a tornado, the top ones tumbling on the floor. At full volume I shouted: "IN MY OPINION, JULIET WAS A WIENER!"

At that moment Mother opened the door.

"Why, Dinah," she said, blinking in bewilderment. "I'm—well, I know I've often encouraged you to develop an interest in classical literature. I just never thought you'd be so...*intense* about it."

**People are getting** *married older, if at all. Don't Madge and Jack read the newspaper?*

*Dinah, I didn't know YOU read the newspaper.*

I was exchanging comments with Pantelli on an Internet chat line. Well, Pantelli had got me on that one. I'd seen a headline about marriage stats on the back of a newspaper someone was holding up at the breakfast buffet a short while ago. I hadn't actually read the story.

I hesitated before punching in a reply on one of the computers in the *Empress Marie*'s dollar-a-minute Internet café. Pantelli would keep me from charging up too many minutes, or rather his schedule would. He had to leave for school in a short while. We'd agreed that each day at breakfast time we'd check in with each other.

*I'm going to sabotage Madge and Jack,* I wrote. *A little time apart would be good for 'em. Sober 'em up.*

*Yeah? How?*

*Dunno yet. Meanwhile, today we go into Skagway.*

*We're booked on the White Pass & Yukon train. Get to see the Klondike, where the Gold Rush was!*

*Cool McCool.*

That was one of Pantelli's expressions. It occurred to me that I was being kind of mean to tell him about the day's, er, Cool McCool sightseeing. By contrast, Pantelli would be heading off to boring old Lord Bithersby. I switched topics.

*Have met some interesting people on the cruise. There's Evan, the pianist, who has this amazing tune, dah DAH dah dah DAH dah, that he can't think of lyrics for. I'm not sure about Evan, though: he might be trying to break into Julie Hébert's room ... Speaking of Julie! You remember her: a cute little thing with spiky hair. Sister of Professor Elaine Hébert, a famous expert on First Nations culture. Well, Elaine may be famous, but she's nasty. Dumps all over Julie, all the time. Squashes Julie's self-confidence!*

Pantelli's reply streamed back to me: *I should ask The Tone about Elaine. He's heard her speak. He was telling us about it at breakfast one day. Or was it dinner?*

The Tone—that is, Pantelli's older brother—Tony, was a high school senior.

*Must've been breakfast. I seem to remember eggs Benedict.*

I typed back, *My name isn't Benedict. Anyhow, forget about your family meals, Pantelli. The Raven's been stolen! The thief,* I added, punching the keys extra hard for emphasis, not that Pantelli could tell this, *is gooseberry-eyed.*

*Well, sounds like Jack is starry-eyed over Madge if he's planning to get hitched to her. HA HA HA.*

Scowling at the screen, I bashed the keys loudly for a snide sign-off: *Enjoy school.*

Clicks echoed in the café. Just how loudly *had* I been typing? Hold on. I wasn't the only customer. The top of a head showed over the computer on the other side of mine.

A head of crisp, dark hair—I rose in my seat—with a soulful lock straying over the forehead.

Talbot St. John.

Feeling a pair of wide, displeased eyes on him, Talbot looked up. We gaped at each other.

His face burned brick-red. Punching in a final key, Talbot gave me a pained grimace of a smile and strode out of the café.


**"I like that!"** announced the young woman behind the counter, in a tone that said plainly she didn't like it at all.

It was the pinch-faced sales clerk from the perfume boutique. "Oh yes," she nodded, recognizing me too, "you'll find me filling in at shops and restaurants all over the ship. They wouldn't give me a job of my own," the young woman added bitterly. "I'm a *fill-in*."

I thought of how I'd got this weeklong singing job on the *Empress*. "I'm a fill-in too," I said. "It's not that bad. You get a free cruise out of it."

And instantly I felt guilty about having written the snide *enjoy school* to Pantelli.

"It's fine for you," the fill-in woman sniffed. "You get applauded. I get snubbed. See?" She shoved a huge, chocolate-sprinkled, whipped-cream-crowned mug across the counter. "Kid orders a triple mocha—and *walks out*."

She was fixing me with an accusing stare, as if I, also being a kid, bore responsibility for what Talbot had done. Well, I supposed in a way I did.

I stammered, "Oh...um, I guess...sure. I would love to drink it. Num. I mean, look how cleverly you've sprinkled the chocolate on." Anything to coax that wounded self-pity off her face.

I wandered round the café, wondering what I was going to do with the triple mocha. I was already stuffed from the breakfast buffet. Maybe there was a plant I could pour the mocha into.

It wasn't a plant my eyes lit on, but the computer Talbot had been using. Whatever key he'd punched, in his hurry to leave, hadn't been an exit command, though I was sure he'd intended it to be. His Hotmail account was still open.

I was about to do the responsible thing and close it for him. Then I noticed the names on his Inbox messages. Most of the names belonged to boys in our class.

One didn't. To me it stood out as if in neon lights. Sickly, garish neon lights.

*Liesl Dubuque*.

The subject line read: *You'll laugh about that tree freak Pantelli ...*

I clicked on the message. Liesl ranted on and on about how Pantelli had been late in from recess because he'd got immersed in studying the bark of a maple tree through his magnifying glass. *What an idiot!* Liesl scoffed.

This wasn't a surprise to me. I knew Liesl sneered at Pantelli for being fascinated with trees. Just like she sneered at me for being loud.

There was just something horrid about seeing her contempt for my buddy set down in print.

Who was Liesl to find other people weird? So Pantelli's hobby was studying trees. Liesl's was twisting and tugging at her wedge of hair. Like, come on.

The responsible thing would have been to adopt a stiff upper lip and shut down the Hotmail on Talbot's behalf.

I wiggled my upper lip. Nope, nothing stiff about it. Besides, I was hatching a scathingly cunning plan.

"Boo-wa-ha-ha," I said, in imitation of an evil laugh. "A plan, Liesl the Weasel. And I'm going to carry it out."

The fill-in woman caught the last part. "You can't carry that triple mocha out," she said, peeved. "I put it in an *Empress Marie* mug. No one told me this was a take-out order."

Eyes welling with tears, Fill-In clip-clopped up to me in very high, very spindly heels. She was clutching a drawstring purse with a plump, smiling kitten embroidered on it. A skinny, miserable kitten, I thought unkindly, would have suited her personality far better.

"I don't have time to put the triple mocha in a Styrofoam cup for you," Fill-In complained. "I'm due at the perfume boutique. Maybe you could hang in here till my relief arrives. He's late, as usual."

She clip-clopped out. I hardly noticed. I was putting my creative powers to work. Sneer at Pantelli, would she! I'd show Liesl.

*Hi Liesl,* I replied on Talbot's Hotmail. *Y'know what I fancy? A girl with close-cropped hair. A short do that doesn't compete with my own soulful lock tumbling down my forehead.*

I paused to giggle appreciatively at my wit, then continued: *Yup. A girl with close-cropped hair — well, I'd ask her out to lunch at the Belgian fries place.*

The Belgian fries place was just up the street from our school, on Commercial Drive. You could get fat, spicy wedge fries with all kinds of toppings. The ideal lunch. And perfect for a first date.

*Hope you'll consider it,* I added. *Yours, Talbot.*

"Boo-wa-ha-ha," I said and pressed SEND.

From my own Hotmail account I sent a message to Pantelli detailing my little prank. There's nothing like sharing good entertainment with a friend.

**Okay, so "good" was** probably not the word my principal, Ms. Chen, would use to describe what I'd just done.

My phony e-mail to Liesl could well end up in Ms. Chen's office, I reflected. Being a weasel, Liesl would immediately tattle on me when she figured out the message was phony.

It would be more *when* than *if*. Liesl was smart, in her weaselly way.

I might as well start practicing my apology now. I sauntered out to the deck. Fill-In's relief person, a cheerful guy with freckles, had assured me I could drink my triple mocha outside the café, *Empress* mug or not. I intended to empty the mocha over the side. I was still too stuffed to want it.

There was nobody around. I opened my mouth to begin practicing—when Fill-In's whiny voice floated to me.

"Can you believe it? My relief person wasn't even there. And I was waiting."

Fill-In must be on the deck above me. The *Empress Marie* had several layers of decks, each one wider than the one above. Like a pile of scalloped potatoes, you might say.

Somebody else, another *Empress Marie* staff member, murmured in sympathy.

"I was so irritated," Fill-In complained.

*Irritated*… I paused, my hand above the railing, ready to pour out the now-tepid triple mocha. A chunk of frozen memory was thawing.

I'd been looking through the binoculars at the Mendenhall Glacier Visitors' Center—and I'd seen someone wearing an irritated, baleful expression. Someone who otherwise didn't appear that way at all.

But who, and why? That part of my memory hadn't thawed yet.

"I should find a job somewhere else," Fill-In was sniffling. "Someplace where I'm appreciated."

Realizing it was about time for me to go meet Jack, I tipped the mug.

"Someplace where people don't rain on my parade!"

Splattering sounds and "AAGGGHHH!" screamed Fill-In.

Uh-oh. I'd assumed I was on the lowest deck and she was on the one above. Apparently I'd got that reversed.

"WHO DID THAT?!"

I sped off to change for swimming.

# Chapter 12
*Lavinia makes like a clam*

I arrived at the pool still clutching the mug. In my hurry to get far, far away from Fill-In, I'd forgotten to return it.

Jack reached into his pocket, found a quarter and dropped it in the mug. "Isn't Trotter paying you enough for crooning?" he inquired.

"I'm not laughing at any of your jokes today," I told him disapprovingly. "Not after last night. I just can't believe you want to get married!"

A tanned, middle-aged woman was easing herself into the nearby hot tub. Hearing my words, she glanced from me to Jack, startled. I didn't pay much attention. I was too indignant.

Jack, whose back was to the woman, gave my chin a friendly pinch. "Well, you know my feelings, Dinah. Is it so bad to express how I feel?"

The tanned woman's mouth dropped. I hardly noticed; I was thinking of Madge, not even graduated from high school yet. Okay, so she had less than six weeks to go. The whole idea of Jack stealing my sister away from Mother, Wilfred and me was outrageous. "It's way too soon," I objected.

Jack looked thoughtful. "Maybe you're right. Maybe in a year?" he asked hopefully.

Frozen, the tanned woman mouthed disbelievingly, "A year?"

I glared back at her. Who'd she think she was, eavesdropping on us? *I* was entitled to be upset about the idea of Jack and Madge getting married. It was none of *her* business.

I was so annoyed that I forgot to be squeamish about the water. Setting the *Empress Marie* mug on a patio table, I sat down at pool's edge—at the shallow end, natch—plugged my nose and slipped in.

When I emerged, blowing bubbles furiously the way Jack had instructed, he was regarding me with bemusement.

"Do you want me to take your glasses for you?" he asked kindly.

I did, but I wasn't going to admit it. Not after his behavior.

"I prefer to swim with them on," I said.

Okay, so this wasn't logical. In a small, petty way it was satisfying.

"Uh...all right. Anyhow, before I teach you how to tread water, I just want you to know I'm sorry if I, y'know, alarmed you last night. With the talk about marriage and everything."

I shook my head to try to get the drops off my glasses. I saw that the tanned woman had stepped out of the hot tub and was approaching Jack. I squinted. Her face was contorted with rage. I wondered, What are Jack and Madge's plans to her?

"We'll talk about marriage when I'm thirteen," I told Jack. After all, I thought, my thirteenth birthday was *months* away. An eternity.

The woman stopped behind Jack. She was clenching and unclenching her fists. "Thirteen!" she mouthed.

What was *with* her? However, I then got distracted by the sight of Mr. Trotter, tiptoeing carefully along the pool's edge in a pair of blue-and-white canvas shoes, with matching white pants and a shirt set off by a blue scarf tucked in at the neck.

I forgot about the enraged tanned woman—for the moment.

Mr. Trotter was carrying an *Empress* mug, from which he took a long, delicious slurp before setting it down by mine on the patio table.

I sniffed the scent that was wafting from the mug. I was

always interested in what other people were eating and drinking. "Lemon," I said. "Lemon tea?"

The program director was vaguely annoyed. "Yes, Miss Galloway. But I've come to tell you—"

"You should order a whipped-cream mocha next time," I advised. "And from the fill-in woman. Her morale's kind of low right now." I rested my arms on the edge of the pool and smiled up at him. Time to repair our relationship, I felt. And what better way than to be helpful?

"I can't order anything with whipped cream," Mr. Trotter snapped. He patted his mustache delicately. "It makes these soggy. I have to drag out the wax again, and—oh, I don't want to get into it."

He reached for his mug. Or what he thought was his mug. Picking mine up by mistake, he took a long swig—and ended up spitting out the quarter. "WHO PUT THIS HERE?" he shouted, red-faced.

Jack and I assumed blank expressions. Mr. Trotter wiped his hand against his mouth and continued: "What I was trying to tell you is that there's to be no more talk about Gooseberry Eyes. You're frightening the passengers. There's a rumor circulating about the ship that you," he thrust his mug in my direction, "suspect the mask thief of being the same person who knocked Miss O'Herlihy down at the cruise terminal. And who shoved you in Mendenhall Lake. Yes?"

"*Yes*," I said.

"NO!" Mr. Trotter took a long slurp of his tea to calm himself. "We can't have *Empress Marie* passengers thinking

a crazed stalker is following the ship hundreds of miles
from Vancouver to Alaska. I need you to STOP with the
theories already, young lady. It's one thing after another
with you!"

"She's just a kid," Jack defended me.

Mr. Trotter's mustache curls trembled. "I was a kid
once myself," he huffed. "*I* never caused trouble. I was a
devoted son." He scowled from me to Jack as if daring us
to argue with him.

Jack winked at me teasingly. "I intend to be a devoted
son-*in-law* one day, provided a certain young lady will
have me."

"THAT DOES IT!" the tanned middle-aged woman burst
out. Raising her arms Frankenstein-style, she stalked toward
Jack. "CRADLE-ROBBER!"

And with a *whoomph!*, she pushed him in the pool.

A mini-tidal wave shot up, drenching Mr. Trotter yet
again.

**After my lesson,** I walked along the deck outside the pool.
Laying my palms flat on the air in front of me, I made
circles with my arms, very pleased with myself. I'd actually
treaded water! Hadn't sunk!

Well, aside from that one time I'd started laughing at
the memory of Jack being shoved in the pool. I'd gone
under then.

After thinking about it, Jack said the tanned woman
must've somehow misinterpreted what we were talking

about. Myself, I just thought she should go for therapy. I mean, pushing people into pools! Aggressive or what?

I continued making circles. I couldn't believe it. I, Dinah Galloway, infamous water coward, had swum!

I passed a large room filled with people gesturing just like I was, only more so. They were raising their arms high, and even lifting one leg and then the other.

A banner across the far wall read MEDITATION EXERCISES. Harp music was playing in the background.

"Huh," I commented. Not really my type of thing.

I would've moved on, but then I noticed Lavinia O'Herlihy in the room. Great! I'd been wanting to talk to her.

If wiggling your arms and legs around was all there was to this meditation exercise stuff, I could easily blend in.

Lavinia had her eyes closed. There was a rapt expression on her face.

I sidled over to her, flailed my arms and asked, "When you were on the day trip to Juneau, did you see Gooseberry Eyes again?"

She popped her eyes open. "What? Gooseberry—no, no, I didn't."

I noticed then that the other people were exercising very slowly, floating a hand or foot this way and then that. No *oomph* in what they were doing—hardly exercising at all, in my opinion.

The class wasn't even trying. To show that I, at least, was serious about physical fitness, I hopped from one foot to the other, *stomp, stomp, stomp!*, as well as vigorously windmilling my arms.

"Lavinia, you've got to speak to Captain Heidgarten. Tell him Gooseberry Eyes crashed into you at the cruise ship terminal. Mr. Trotter thinks I'm just causing trouble by talking about Gooseberry Eyes. But the same guy tried to break into my house, I'm sure of it," I puffed, starting to get out of breath.

Lavinia dropped her arms, which she'd been holding up in an arc shape, and glared at me. "The Captain did ask me about that, Dinah Galloway. Most embarrassing it was, too—right in the middle of a bingo game! Dreadful, being stopped and questioned, with everyone listening in." Lavinia drew a deep breath through her nose and scowled at me down the length of it, as if I smelled. "A lady, Dinah Galloway, does not become involved in notoriety!"

I had no idea what notoriety was. Maybe some other game the ship was offering? "But you're involved in bingo," I pointed out.

Lavinia screamed, "THERE WAS NO GOOSE-BERRY EYES! I NEVER SAW HIM! NOW LEAVE ME ALONE!"

The room, not surprisingly, had gone silent. The instructor strode up to me. "You may be the *Empress*'s singing sensation," she snapped, flicking her long, blond hair back so angrily that a couple of her students had to duck. "I guess that gives you a giant ego as well as a giant voice. *Fine*." The instructor turned a blazing pink. "But it does not give you license to intrude on my class and mock us—by *gyrating*."

"Gyrating!" I put down my arms, which, absentmindedly, I'd been continuing to flail about. "Well, that's nice. After I've been trying to set a good example."

She marched me out of the room.

**I stood outside,** doing some meditating of my own. Another chunk of yesterday's icy memory was thawing.

Just now, Lavinia had been pretty mad at me. I realized I'd glimpsed her fury once before. Through binoculars, yesterday afternoon. *She'd* been the person stomping around the Visitors' Center looking irritated and baleful.

What had Lavinia been so upset about?

And today she'd denied Gooseberry Eyes had bumped into her at the cruise ship terminal.

Why was Lavinia suddenly so reluctant to talk?

# Chapter 13

*Musical chairs on the scenic tour*

Mr. Trotter put Mother in charge of the scenic tour tickets, each in an envelope labeled with a passenger's name, to be handed out at the train station. The program director had informed us, with a pointed glance at me, that he was far too stressed to hand out the tickets himself.

Not everyone had signed up for the three-hour tour to the Yukon gold fields. There were lots of shops to explore in Skagway, and friendly locals to greet you in a hearty, cowboy drawl.

It's a Skagway tradition to recite poems to visitors. I stopped and listened to a man with gold teeth intone one that started:

*Skulls, skulls, in the midnight sun,*
*Bleached by snow, every one!*

Now that was my type of poetry. None of this "I wandered lonely as a cloud" stuff that we had to memorize at school.

I grinned at the man. He grinned back, his gold teeth blinding me. I don't know about the midnight sun, but the noonday sun this far north was intense, almost white.

"Come along," urged Mother as I shielded my eyes. "I want to get to the station before everyone else."

She bustled me off. The man called after us:

*Better get sunglasses!*
*Or else be fated to burn*
*In the Gold Rush passes.*

"I wonder if he always speaks in rhymes," said Madge, hurrying along with Jack to keep up with us. "Maybe he's got some kind of syndrome, like the one that makes people swear all the time."

Jack finished her thought. "So instead of swear words pouring out of his mouth, you get rhyming couplets," and they both laughed.

Madge, I saw, was looking very happy. Fresh and bright too, I noticed, glancing over my shoulder at her as Mother rushed us towards the station. Then I realized—Madge wasn't wearing any makeup. No foundation, no eyeliner, nothing. And her hair was up in a plain old ponytail. A first.

Not that Madge needed makeup. Her skin was like porcelain and her eyelashes, framing those brilliant lupine blues, were naturally long and dark.

I remembered Jack's talk with her about not having to be perfect all the time. It had paid off! My sister was finally loosening up.

Wait a minute. Madge being too happy isn't good, I thought. *Too* happy could lead to a wedding. I frowned at Madge and Jack, who were poring over a brochure with a map of the White Pass & Yukon Route train tour we were about to take.

"The White Pass summit is two thousand, eight hundred feet," Jack observed and let out an appreciative whistle. "Hey!" he exclaimed to Madge. "You sure you're going to be all right on this trip? The train really barrels along, and on a pretty narrow track. I mean, with your, uh, your—"

"Tendency to throw up?" Madge supplied. She smiled at him. "Know what? You've been very therapeutic for me. After we had our talk last night, I didn't throw up once."

"I think I'm about to, though," I muttered.

"About to what?" inquired Mother. She gave me a harried look over the shoebox full of tickets she was carrying.

"Dinah, you've got this odd habit of mumbling to yourself. I'd reprimand you for it, except I know you inherited it from me. It used to drive your father crazy... Here, you keep this, dear," she thrust the box into my hands, "and I'll check people off on this clipboard as they pick up their tickets. Yes, good plan, Suzanne," Mother mumbled to herself.

I sat down on the bench, the shoebox on my lap. "Dah DAH dah dah DAH dah," I sang. "The TRAIN on the TRAIN track... Hey, will Evan be on the tour?"

"No, he's staying on the ship." Mother shrugged. "Wants to work on his song. Says he can't enjoy excursions when he's trying to think of lyrics."

*Phhht!* I ran my fingertips along the tops of the envelopes. Evan might have another reason for not going on tours. A sinister one. It had sure been suspicious the way he snuck down to Julie's door when he knew she was busy playing volleyball. Maybe he intended to prowl around some more.

"STUFF AND NONSENSE!"

I jumped. Ira Stone was beside me.

He chuckled. "Frightened you, did I? Hee-hee!"

I retorted good-naturedly, "Hee-hee, yourself."

Mother gave me a slight frown for being uppity, as she would say, with an adult. Remembering my duties, I flipped through the envelopes to the one labeled STONE, IRA and handed it to him.

The effort of chuckling had shaken Ira's thin frame; the cane he was leaning on wobbled this way and that, as if caught in a strong wind. Concerned he'd topple, I shot out a hand to steady the cane.

*Empress Marie* passengers started approaching Mother. Ira whispered to me, "Could you do me a favor, young 'un? Seat me somewhere else on the train than beside Lavinia O'Herlihy. She got Trotter to put us side by side. Thing is, I can't stand the woman—she's always nagging me about what a good wife she'd make."

The effort of speaking was also too much for Ira. He broke into a series of racking coughs. I edged down the bench, away from him. The guy must be unleashing germs by the battalion—and he was not, I noticed in Mother-like disapproval, covering his mouth when he coughed.

Me, Mother-like! Holy Toledo. I'd better watch that.

Still, I did feel sorry for Ira. I didn't blame him for feeling annoyed, with Lavinia trailing after him all the time.

"Sure, I'll change her seat." I flipped through the envelopes, *pfft! pfft!* "Here she is. O'HERLIHY, LAVINIA."

The first few passengers, checked off by Mother on her list, were waiting behind Ira for their tickets. Among them: Jack and Madge.

Hmmm. Mother had arranged for all of us to sit together...

Maybe if Jack and Madge didn't spend *quite* so much time with each other, they wouldn't be thinking about the possibility of FRENCH, MADGE.

"Boo-wa-ha-ha," I said, pleased with this, my second scathingly cunning plan of the day. Was I on a roll, or what?

Rapidly I switched Lavinia's ticket into Madge's envelope and vice versa. I winked at Ira. "Boo-wa-ha-ha."

"Hee-hee!"


**When the tickets** in the shoebox had thinned to just a few, Mother told Madge, Jack and me to go ahead and take our seats on the train. She'd be right there herself.

"I might buy some sunglasses," Madge said, surveying a rack of them in a nearby shop. "I forgot mine on the ship, and people keep talking about how bright the snow will be out the train windows."

She waved aside our offer to wait for her. "It'll take me a minute or two. I have to find just the right hue of frames so the glasses won't clash with my hair."

I lifted my eyebrows at Jack. My sister was getting more relaxed about herself—but she was still fussy.

The tanned, middle-aged woman from the pool was already in her seat—right in front of Jack. "Ah," said Jack, as her features, going red, took on the appearance of a sunburn as opposed to a tan. He remarked to her, "If I'd known you'd be close by, I'd have brought a towel."

In the seats across the aisle from Jack, where Mother would be joining me, I snorted appreciatively.

The woman burned even redder. "I—I misunderstood about the girl you're hoping to marry. I thought she was," the woman avoided looking at me, "much younger than you."

Though the tanned woman wasn't including me in the conversation, I saw no reason not to jump in. After all,

Madge was my sister. "No way she's much younger than Jack!" I exclaimed, reflecting that Madge was only two years Jack's junior. Incredible to believe Madge would be graduating from high school in a month. "I can't imagine being as old as she is," I added, shaking my head.

Jack laughed. "You're making my one-and-only sound like an aged crone, Dinah. I think there's a bit of life left in the old girl."

I airily waved a hand at the tanned woman. "Yeah, you'll see her in a minute. She'll be sitting right beside Jack."

I stopped in horror. No, Madge *wouldn't* be sitting right beside Jack. I'd switched her ticket. It'd be Lavinia who'd plop down beside him.

"Uh-oh," I said and put on my phony bared-teeth smile. It was the only course of action I could come up with.

Jack didn't notice. His gray eyes were twinkling with amusement. "The 'old thing' I hope to marry some day should be along pretty soon," he assured the tanned woman.

It was then that Lavinia O'Herlihy, frowning in puzzlement at her ticket, walked up and slid into the seat beside Jack...

**Madge just made it** on in time. She was explaining to Mother that she'd had trouble choosing between brands of sunglasses when the conductor asked her to take her seat. Glancing at her ticket, he instructed, "Down there, Miss," and pointed a dozen or so rows along to the empty seat beside Ira.

"But—but—" Madge, Jack and Lavinia protested.

"Please, Miss," the conductor said.

It was the kind of "please" you didn't refuse. Madge moved to the empty seat. Above her, bright brass luggage racks reflected, one after another, the burnished red of her hair.

It wouldn't be such a bad trip for Madge, I decided. Ira was snoozing, his head against the window, his mouth slightly open. Yup, I thought. It'd be a nice, *single* experience for Madge.

**The train skimmed** along the banks of the roiling Skagway River. Boy! I had the feeling that if I could reach out and touch that angry current, it would slap back.

The train trundled past gorges with wide, dazzling mountains of ice. Their jagged peaks loomed so high I had to press the top of my head against the window and squint up to see. With the sun on them, the peaks sent off brilliant flashes. Even with clip-on sunglasses, my eyes hurt, but it was worth it.

"Whoa," moaned Lavinia as we wound past a deep, surging, silver waterfall that sent up white clouds of spray. Beneath her horn-rimmed sunglasses, Lavinia's face sagged.

"Of course, you wouldn't be trainsick if you sat farther back," Jack advised Lavinia. "It's well known that the front seats are much harder on the stomach. Maybe we should switch you with, say, Madge."

Ooooo, crafty.

However, Jack would have to wait a while before exchanging Lavinia for Madge. A lot of people on his side, that is, the right one, were standing to peer out the windows on my side. There was just a better view on the left. Jack wouldn't be able to escort Lavinia past for now.

I began to chuckle out my evil "Boo-wa-ha-ha" when I noticed one of the people standing nearby. Talbot St. John—holding on to the luggage rack so he could bend down to see out without falling into someone's lap. He was wearing a CD player and headphones. Huh! I bet he was the type who listened to doofus trendy bands.

He noticed me at the same time and reddened. Scowling at Talbot, I raised the current Deathstalkers comic book to block him out.

"Enjoy reading upside down, do you?"

It was Captain Heidgarten's jolly voice. I lowered the Deathstalkers, who were indeed on their heads while firing stingrays, laser guns, etc., at assorted enemies. I closed the comic book and grinned at the Captain. Talbot had edged down the aisle and out of sight. "I'm not really reading," I assured him.

"I should hope not!" he returned, beaming. "I sign up for the White Pass & Yukon Route every time we anchor at Skagway. Never grow tired of it. Why, look at that…"

I looked. Straight down and down and—

"Whoa!" moaned Lavinia.

Captain Heidgarten said cheerfully, "We're high up, all right—a thousand feet high, as a matter of fact, on a wooden trestle bridge. Don't see too many of 'em anymore—they probably violate about three dozen safety regulations."

The Captain and I laughed heartily. Not everyone appreciated his robust sailor's humor, though. A few people, Lavinia included, turned ashen.

**However, Captain Heidgarten** soon distracted us all with the story of Jefferson "Soapy" Smith of Klondike Gold Rush fame.

Soapy got his nickname in Denver, Colorado, where he tricked people into buying expensive bars of soap. He claimed each bar had a hundred-dollar bill at the center. "Not exactly good, clean fun," remarked Captain Heidgarten.

Soapy was attracted to the chance of fast money, so he hotfooted it to the Klondike. Only he didn't make his profits there by hunting for gold. Instead, Soapy set up a fake telegraph office. He got chummy with the successful prospectors, then presented them with phony telegrams from loved ones pleading for money.

He must've been slick as a wet bar of soap, all right. The worried prospectors shoved bags of money at Soapy. They just assumed he'd send it to their families for them. Which, of course, he didn't.

From a few seats behind me, Julie Hébert piped up. "So he was charming *and* cunning." She saw me craning round at her and winked. "Just like the Raven."

I felt slightly offended on the Raven's behalf. After all, the legendary bird had a nice side. It didn't sound like Jefferson "Soapy" Smith'd had so much as a nice *particle*.

On the other hand, at least Julie's spirits were picking up. Since the theft of the mask, she'd been anxious and pale.

Captain Heidgarten nodded at Julie. "Soapy was charming, cunning...and not that long-lived. Eventually some angry locals came after him and—well, let's just say that Soapy's luck went down the drain."

**The train route** included two tunnels. I like tunnels because you can gulp in your breath at the beginning and hold it till you're outside again. Mother and Madge find this gross, but the challenge is actually very fun and satisfying.

Not far into the first tunnel, a sharp, pointy object jabbed me in the side—followed by a cackle. I was startled into letting my breath out. Lavinia! The pointy object had been her elbow.

As I was massaging my side, a whiff of Chanel No. 5 floated past. The train whished out of the tunnel. In the seat across from me, Madge was now sitting beside Jack.

I glanced back. Lavinia was with Ira. She was applying her sharp elbow to *his* side, to wake him up. Poor guy. I guessed he was in for another lecture about what a great wife she'd be.

"Smooth," I congratulated Jack.

He bowed to me. "Thank you, Modom."

Madge, though, was not taking the situation with good humor. "That horrible old man snored," she informed me, her blue eyes several degrees colder than the ice gorge we were passing. "And he was snoring out the smell of onions. Yech!" she shuddered.

"You're responsible for this, Dinah Mary Galloway," Madge went on. My sister was not the type to let a prank go by lightly. "Oh no, don't deny it."

Then I forgot about Madge, who proceeded to scold Jack that there was nothing to laugh at. Outside Mother's and my window, eagles were swooping and skyrocketing. Mother and I watched them as, below, just-blossoming elderberry bushes pushed out their creamy, star-shaped flowers, and plump, chocolate-colored wolverines bent their white foreheads and bustled hastily away from the train into the woods.


**At the second tunnel**, undistracted, I held my breath from beginning to end. When we emerged, my cheeks were still puffed out with the air I was holding in. Several seats ahead, Talbot was leaning on his armrest — and his cheeks were puffed out too. *He'd* been doing the same thing!

He happened to glance back, and for a second we stared at each other with our faces bloated, jellyfish-style.

Then, annoyed that somebody else was on to this holding-your-breath-in-a-tunnel routine, which I'd thought was my invention, I drew back out of sight. I let my breath out with a loud *bwwwccck*, like the deflating sound of a balloon. This was also part of the routine.

I looked across at Madge, hoping for an annoyed reaction. The *bwwwccck* was usually good for one.

Madge wasn't paying any attention. After being in the tunnel, she was rosy-cheeked and smiling. She did cast a couple of scolding frowns at Jack, but these were definitely pretend ones. Post-smooch pretend ones, in fact.

Brother, I thought.

Huh! But not brother-*in-law*, not for a long time, I vowed.

# Chapter 14

## The true snakewoman, revealed

First thing next morning on our Internet chat line, I punched in opening remarks to Pantelli. *You wouldn't believe what we saw yesterday on the train tour!*

He cut in: *You wouldn't believe what we saw yesterday at Lord Bithersby. Liesl the Weasel got her hair chopped! Now she looks like a burned match—pale and skinny, with just a bit of black at the top. You fooled her with that phony e-mail message, Di. She's bragging to everyone that Talbot's gonna take her out for a Belgian fries lunch date! HA HA HA.*

I didn't view the outcome of my prank quite so merrily as Pantelli. I foresaw a long—make that Rip Van Winkle's lifetime-long—session in the principal's office. How could Liesl have fallen for that phony e-mail? Stupidity?

No. Vanity, I decided. Only a girl as stuck-up and conceited as Liesl Dubuque would believe a twelve-year-old boy would write her such a mushy message.

*I hope you didn't tell her anything*, I typed.

*Me? No way! Your secret is safe with yours truly. Liesl will never weasel out of me that you're the culprit.*

*Phew*, I wrote. I wished, though, that Pantelli wouldn't use the word "culprit." It sounded so...criminal.

*Yeah, all I did was walk up to Liesl, point to her hair and laugh deafeningly.*

Great, I thought. Like sharp-witted Liesl won't figure out now that I'm involved. *Thanks a lot, Pantelli,* I wrote.

*You're welcome!*

My face was scrunched up in dismay. "Bad news?" said Fill-In hopefully. She set down the double mocha I'd ordered. It was the first time I'd ever seen a hint of cheer, however wan, on Fill-In. I guessed other people's disappointments were the only thing that improved her spirits.

"Sort of bad," I admitted.

I'd been right. Fill-In's pencil-thin eyebrows went up and her pinched features splintered into a crack of a smile.

Julie Hébert strolled into the Internet café. She, too, noticed my face. "I don't think I'll order what Dinah's drinking," Julie joked to Fill-In.

I giggled. Fill-In, interpreting this as an insult, shriveled up her smile again. "I'm not appreciated. And my replacement's late again. I hate being kept waiting." She grabbed a blue napkin with a fat white ship imprinted on it and blew her nose.

"I'll have a cappuccino, please," Julie called to Fill-In.

Pantelli typed, *Hey, are you still there, Di?*

*Yeah,* I replied. *It's just that Julie Hébert showed up.*

*Oh, right. Julie. Turns out The Tone has seen Julie himself. She made quite the impression on him and his classmates.*

Julie walked over to the counter to pay Fill-In. "Would you like a chocolate biscotti to go with your mocha, Dinah?" she offered, smiling. "My treat." She gestured to a glass canister crammed with goodies. "Or maybe a chocolate fudge brownie?"

Madge may have dawdled over fashion decisions, but for me the choice of biscotti versus brownie was the difficult type. "Um," I said, wondering if it would be rude to ask for *both*. "Ummmm..."

More words from Pantelli flowed across the screen. *The Tone said that in the middle of a lecture at the Roundhouse Community Center, Julie stormed in and threw a tantrum!*

I gaped at the screen. *Huh?* I typed. *That's not how I heard it from Julie.*

I realized Julie was waiting for my reply. "I think I'll have a..."

My attention faded. I was concentrating on Pantelli's next message.

*Yeah, Julie screeched at Elaine that she couldn't possibly live on the allowance Elaine gave her. The costs of having a private trainer, plus her weekly visit to the beauty salon, were draining all her pocket money, Julie said. Not only that, but it was totally unfair of Elaine to buy Julie a new car only every three years—Julie was missing out on the latest gizmos.*

"Impossible," I said, dazed. This was Julie? My Julie?

"You'll have an 'impossible'?" Julie questioned good-humoredly. Fill-In, tongs poised over the biscotti and brownies, gave an angry sniff.

"I ... " Slumping in my seat, I gazed stupidly at Pantelli's words. They just kept pouring out, unstoppable as toothpaste when you've squeezed the tube too hard.

*The Tone says Julie then whined about having to clean their house. "Yeah, I know I'm the one who trashed it, but I was upset," Julie shouted. The Tone, sitting nearby, had to dodge her spit drops.*

I responded weakly, *You mean—Julie lives with Elaine? I thought she was suffering in some dive on Cadwallader Avenue.*

*Not from what The Tone gathered. This is one weird dame, Di. She finished by demanding a check for some art class she wanted to take—then slammed out of the room. Professor Hébert burst into tears. "I'm sorry," she sniffed. "I've—I've tried so hard with my stepsister—given her everything."*

"Everything," I repeated numbly.

"Everything?" Julie questioned. Her smile didn't waver. "Isn't that a teeny bit greedy, Dinah?"

What a soft voice Julie had, I thought suddenly. Not that I hadn't noticed before, but it occurred to me now just how very soft it was. Like a snake's hiss...

"I..." I mumbled.

"Yes, Dinah?"

"I think I've lost my appetite," I said weakly.

I wandered onto the volleyball court. Nobody was around to play. Most passengers were heading out to Ketchikan, our port of the day. Mother, Madge and I were waiting for Jack to be off-duty at noon, and then we'd be going.

I pulled on the netting and let it bounce into place. I decided to repeat this a few times. It was kind of fun. The harder I tugged, the more fiercely the net whipped back.

I'm what you'd call one of those creative kids who can be left to their own gifted resources.

Besides, fidgeting helped my thought processes. Julie was a phony! From what The Tone said, *she* was the nasty Hébert, not Elaine. Imagine complaining because you weren't bought a new car every three years! Heck, if you were a Galloway, you got a new *used* one every fifteen years.

In my frustration at having been fooled, I yanked the netting even farther back. Quite a stretch—just like Julie's sob stories.

I thought of the cell-phone call. The one at my house, where Elaine had assumed I was Julie. And had been so nasty.

Hadn't she?

I reconsidered the conversation. Elaine had insisted Julie keep cleaning. I'd thought that was mean, especially at dinnertime—but if Julie had trashed the house, well, duh. Of course Julie ought to be tidying up.

Julie had stretched that one cleaning job into the yarn that she had to earn her keep at Elaine's as a cleaning woman.

It sure sounded like Julie was the type to chew up facts and spit them out in a twisted form. Twisted—like those snakes curling from Medusa's head.

Yech. I shuddered. The inside of Julie's mind was not a place I'd like to visit.

On the other hand, Elaine had definitely forbidden Julie to talk to people about the mask. *You know nothing*, she'd snapped over the phone.

These Hébert sisters—what a pair! I was sure glad Madge and I weren't like them. Julie and Elaine made us seem semi-normal.

**I trudged off,** then stopped. Yawning at my feet were the stairs down to Julie Hébert's room.

And coming up the stairs was Evan Brander, who immediately went scarlet. "W-what are you doing here?"

*He* was questioning *me* about being here? I narrowed my eyes into what I hoped were forbidding hazel slits. "What are *you* doing here?"

"L-look, Dinah. There's something I haven't been quite up-front about." After giving his lower lip a nervous chew, Evan opened his mouth to stammer out what was doubtless a sordid confession.

Just then—"Greetings!" It was the friendly steward I'd met last time by these stairs. He bore a fresh stack of fluffy blue towels imprinted with fat white ships.

Startled, Evan fled up the stairs.

"Jittery type," commented the steward.

"He has a guilty conscience about something," I informed the steward darkly and then sighed. "I always have trouble with my pianists."

I went downstairs with the steward because I didn't know what else to do. I was feeling kind of stunned. First, I'd found out that Julie was a whopping liar. Second, more proof that Evan was up to no good.

The steward knocked on doors. No one answered any of them. Nobody stays in a stateroom much on a cruise ship, unless, like Madge, they're barfing. The steward was able to pop in and distribute towels.

"Room service!" he called through Julie's door. No reply, so he unlocked it with his pass key.

"Bet she's gone ashore to Ketchikan," he told me. "Was it something urgent?"

He assumed I wanted to speak to Julie. Ha! With what

I'd found out, I'd happily stay away from the lady for several lifetimes. Our truth-stretching Julie was—let's all make like a sheep now—ba-a-a-ad news.

I was about to pooh-pooh the steward's assumption when I noticed the hairclip I'd loaned Julie on the chest of drawers. The elegant, cat-shaped hairclip Madge had made specially for me.

Hmph! Well, I'd reclaim that in no time flat. A snake-shaped hairclip—now that'd suit Julie.

"I'll just grab my hairclip, if that's okay," I said.

The steward laughed. "You should adopt my hairdo, kid." He pointed at his very unmessy hair—a crew cut. "No need for hairclips!"

After depositing some towels in the bathroom, the steward said, "Go ahead. Just remember to shut the door when you're through."

He pounded on the next door down the hall. "Room service!" he yelled.

"C'mon in," said a voice—a sort of familiar voice, but I headed into Julie's room and forgot about it.

**I grabbed the hairclip** and would have left—except that Julie's painting of Medusa, now taped to the wall, caught my glance. And trapped it, as if I, like Medusa's victims, had been turned to stone. The painting was so gruesome, it was fascinating. Kind of like anchovies, if you know what I mean.

Medusa leered out at me, eyes crazed and lips shrunken back over sharp teeth. "Ewww," I told her.

I looked more closely at that wild face and snaky hair. There was something familiar about Medusa. I couldn't quite place it...

For a closer squint at the painting, I grasped the bottom two corners, which weren't taped to the wall, and pulled them toward me. I'd seen this creepy woman before, I was sure of it!

I couldn't figure out where.

I let go of the two corners—and realized my right thumb had come away wet. I examined it. Smeared with paint! Well, I did remember Julie saying Medusa was a work-in-progress. More like a *yech*-in-progress, if you ask me.

Ideally Julie wouldn't notice a smudge in the bottom right-hand corner, where *Medusa, by Julie Hébert* had been. If Julie did notice the smudge, she'd just have to repaint it, that was all.

Wait—the words were still there after all. Except for "Medusa." I'd rubbed that off to reveal another word, the original word, underneath.

*Elaine*.

**Whoa. Talk about** your unflattering likeness. Julie had painted this horrid Medusa as a portrait of her sister! No wonder Medusa seemed familiar to me. It was the Hébert family resemblance.

Even if Elaine *was* uppity with her sister, she didn't deserve this. What a hateful way for Julie to portray her.

Then, breathily, through the open stateroom door: "Are you finished with my room, steward?"

Julie! Boy, that'd been a fast visit to Ketchikan.

"Yes, ma'am, I'm finished," came the steward's cheery voice. "The door's open cuz your little buddy had to retrieve her hairclip. She must've scooted off—sorry, I *did* ask her to close the door. Aw, well, you know how kids are."

"My little—you mean Dinah Galloway?" The whispery voice had a sudden forked-tongue-like sharpness to it.

Julie, I thought, was the true snakewoman.

I gulped. A snakewoman who might have an eagle eye—to spot, for example, the freshly wiped-off name *Elaine* on her painting.

Snakes, eagles...Enough with the animal analogies, Dinah. Julie was pushing the stateroom door wider open. Time for quick but rational action—

I dove under the bed.

**Squashed in the narrow** space under the bed, I was regretting all those buffets. Why hadn't I been dainty, like Madge, and filled my plate with half grapefruits and slivers of cantaloupe?

My cat, Wilfred, would have loved it here, but I was waiting in agony for Julie to leave. I could only manage half breaths, at best.

She seemed in no hurry to go. I heard her rustling the brochures; then, horrors, she plunked down on the bed.

*Oof!* I foresaw myself sliding out from under the bed later on, flattened into a coin and rolling out to the hall before the surprised gaze of the steward.

*Ping, ping!* Julie was punching in cell-phone numbers. Great, a long, cozy chat with someone.

Julie didn't bother with greetings. "I'm going to be a bit late," she said into the phone. "I left my wallet behind. Had to come back. You're at the Blandish Arms Hotel? ... There's a coffee shop? ... Good, I could use a particularly strong cup about now ... No, there's no problem at this end, except for our nosy, sleuthing songbird."

A nosy, sleuthing songbird. Ah. That would be me.

"Pity you let her mother see your eyes when you grabbed the Raven ... Oh, I know, I know, you couldn't help it. But your eyes are so, er, distinctive."

Holy Toledo! Julie was talking to — *Gooseberry Eyes*. She was in league with him!

My jaw would have thudded to the floor if it hadn't already been jammed up against it.

"Forget Mrs. Galloway," Julie soothed into the cell phone. "I needed a witness, someone who'd vouch that the Raven was wrestled away from me. Suzanne makes the perfect witness. A mom. An upstanding citizen. No one would doubt her judgment."

Julie gave a luxurious sigh. "With the proceeds of the mask, I can set up my own gallery. Just think of our oh-so-rosy future. You can help me run my gallery if you like. All I need is a chance to show my paintings to the world!" Julie's voice grew whiny. "It's so unfair that I haven't had one."

Then the whining tone changed to a scornful laugh. "Amusing to think of the Juneau police bumbling about, trying to find the mask—those fools haven't the faintest hint!"

This can't get any worse, I thought in disgust.

It got worse. Julie put more of her weight on the bed. Her feet swung out of view; she was leaning. I heard her scrabble in the night-table drawer.

I couldn't help it. A squeak escaped me. Or was that my bones crunching?

"Now don't start complaining," Julie snapped into the phone. "...Oh yes you were. I heard you. You *bleated*."

She listened for a moment and, in reply, her tone grew wheedling. "Okay, okay, don't get huffy. I know you're putting in lots of hours as a fence."

By "fence" somehow I didn't think Julie meant the picket kind. Gooseberry Eyes was evidently touring around Alaska, a sort of illegal traveling salesman, trying to sell the Raven.

"But leave the decisions to me, okay?" Julie scolded. "For instance, I couldn't believe you showed up in the cruise ship terminal, and at the bottom of the gangway, yet, thinking we'd have time for a pre-cruise chat! Were you out of your mind? And did you have to be clumsy during every single fake-theft attempt? It gets so tiresome!...I know, I know, your mother didn't give you enough dairy products as a child, and your bones are weak. But shoving our little songbird into the lake—totally unnecessary, and a stupid risk, besides... Well, never mind. Concentrate on finding a buyer for us. You're the expert on who the buyers are here. It's your home state."

With a *ping!* Julie shut off her cell phone. She rose abruptly. Her feet proceeded with springy, athletic strides to the door. Then she was gone.

**There was a ripping** sound as I slid from under the bed. Too bad I'd pulled on one of Madge's sweatshirts this morning. My sister was so fussy about the state of her clothes. On the other hand, Madge *had* seemed to relax a bit on this trip. Maybe she wouldn't mind a weeny tear.

However, Madge's moods were the last thing on my mind right now. Julie was just as mixed up in the mask theft as Gooseberry Eyes! And every time the *Empress Marie* docked, Julie popped ashore to meet Gooseberry Eyes and discuss how the fencing of the mask was going.

I had to tell Captain Heidgarten right away.

# Chapter 15
## The Raven and the professor

I tried not to talk too rapidly, as I do when I'm excited. "Julie's been in cahoots with Gooseberry Eyes all along. She pretended to be worried about the mask's safety while planning with Gooseberry Eyes to steal it!"

I snapped my fingers—and noticed the bitten-off ends were starting to grow in again. Well, I'd tend to personal hygiene later.

I continued, as Captain Heidgarten regarded me with his bright blue eyes and Mr. Trotter spluttered. "In the phone call I overheard, Julie mentioned that Alaska was Gooseberry Eyes' 'home state.' That's why he *faked* a few attempted thefts in Vancouver. This is where his fencing contacts are."

By now Mr. Trotter was gaping as well as flushing. "Do—do you know you have a spring sticking out of your back?"

I stretched a hand round and felt a coil shape. *Boing!* "It's a bedspring," I said impatiently. "Look, Mr. T., I think we should stay focused, okay?

"Now the *painting*," I said to Captain Heidgarten. "The ultra-yechy painting of Medusa. Julie thinks it's a brilliant work—anyone else can tell it's ghastly! The only value of the painting, in my opinion, is that it tells us how Julie sees Elaine. Julie's jealous of Elaine's success and fame. Julie thinks the success and fame should be *hers*."

More spluttering from Mr. Trotter. I decided it was best to ignore him, even though it sounded as if he was about to erupt like Mount St. Helens.

I said, "Julie kept telling us how artistic she was, and how interested she was in myths of different cultures. But she was also complaining about Elaine. This bothered me, and not just because it got so boring. Why would somebody as intelligent as Julie use up so much time griping?

"I mean," and to help myself think it through, I began swinging my feet, *ponk, ponk, ponk*, against the front of Captain Heidgarten's mahogany desk, "I'd watch Julie's face while she went on and on about Elaine. The words coming out of Julie didn't match the sweet, patient person she was supposed to be. It was as if..."

*Ponk, ponk, ponk!* Any other grown-up would have told me off by now for inflicting furniture damage, but the Captain's bright blue eyes gleamed with understanding. He finished for me: "As if she'd been wearing a mask all along."

"Yes!" I said.

"No," moaned Mr. Trotter. By now he was so hot with agitation that his mustache curls were starting to droop.

Captain Heidgarten frowned at him. "Lionel, for heaven's sake, get a grip."

The program director looked wildly about as if wondering where this grip might be. In the meantime, Captain Heidgarten dragged a Vancouver telephone directory from a mahogany cabinet. He flipped over great chunks of pages until "Ah, here we are. University of British Columbia … let's see, History Department … "

He punched in the number and switched on his speakerphone.

"Good day," said a stilted English voice. "This is the History—"

"Right," interrupted Captain Heidgarten. "Can you please tell me how to get in touch with Professor Elaine Hébert?"

**"Sightseeing!"** I objected as Captain Heidgarten propelled me rather forcibly along by the elbow. "The sight I want to see is Julie Hébert getting nabbed, along with her co-conspirator, Gooseberry Eyes, at the Blandish Arms Hotel."

I also wanted to see the arrival of Elaine Hébert, who, in the wake of Captain Heidgarten's call, was flying up right away from her dig in northern B.C. Would Elaine clobber Julie? This could be interesting.

"Best leave it to the police," Captain Heidgarten said, with annoying good humor. "Let them apprehend Julie at the Blandish Arms."

After contacting the prof, Captain Heidgarten had phoned the police. Hadn't let me talk to them, though—not that I wasn't signaling wildly enough for his attention. In fact, with a frightened look at my gyrating arms, Mr. Trotter had covered his mustache protectively and scurried from the office.

Now Captain Heidgarten said, "Why, looky. There's your friend, about to go ashore too."

I surveyed the people his big, sun-bronzed hand was waving towards. I didn't know any of them, except—oh, he *couldn't* mean...

"Talbot St. John?!" I said in deep disgust.

There was a crisp breeze on deck, and unfortunately it whisked my words right over to Talbot. He turned and for a second stared at me from under that soulful forelock.

"Yup, I saw you two eyeing each other on the train yesterday," Captain Heidgarten went on playfully. "Adolescent crushes, eh?"

Talbot turned back to his mother, whose stiffly sprayed hair was resisting the breeze like an army helmet.

"You are so-o-o wrong," I informed Captain Heidgarten.

"In fact, just for *saying* that, you should be made to walk the plank."

He laughed. I did not join him.

We reached Mother, Madge and Jack, who were waiting for me by the gangway. Captain Heidgarten summed up the Julie situation for them in a way that was both terse and reassuring. A good, Captainly way, I thought with approval — though I was still cross with him.

Their little meeting ended with Mother, Madge and Jack all agreeing to spirit me off for a busy afternoon of touristing.

"I wanted to help stake out the Blandish Arms," I fumed as Captain Heidgarten strolled away.

Mother and Madge looked horrified, but Jack laughed. He pulled at the spring sticking out of the back of the sweatshirt I was wearing and let it *boing!* "I believe the idea of a stakeout is to have people waiting in absolute stillness and quiet for a prolonged period of time. That would disqualify *you*, Dinah-mite."

"Dinah might not survive until the stakeout anyway," remarked Madge, her eyes thinning into baleful blue slits. "That happens to be my cerise sweatshirt she's ruined."

" 'Cerise'!" I exclaimed. "Is that like baseball? Like, the World Cerise?"

It was raining in Ketchikan. Mother enfolded me in a bright yellow plastic poncho, which made me feel like a rubber duck.

Ketchikan gets a 162 inches of rain a year, making it the wettest city in southern Alaska. Jack announced in a know-it-all way that Vancouver, known for *its* rain, only gets forty-nine inches a year.

"Who cares? It's just water," I shrugged. I was still in a bad mood about being excluded from the stakeout.

"That's what I could have said to you a few days ago about swimming," Jack said, smiling. "When you were afraid of 'just water.' Now you're treading water like a pro. Today, Jack French's swimming class. Tomorrow, the Olympics."

I ignored him, even though the compliment pleased me. In the cab we got into, I traced the word UNFAIR on the fogged-up window. Why *couldn't* I help catch Julie and her co-conspirator, Gooseberry Eyes?

Then it occurred to me that "unfair" was what Julie Hébert had gone around saying all the time she was on the *Empress*. I didn't want to end up like her, too busy envying other people's lives to lead one of her own.

So I turned around and joined the others' conversation. Their oo's and ah's, anyway. We were passing the galleries and shops of the famous, once very wild-west-ish Creek Street, whose wooden houses were painted so vibrantly their colors shone, even in the rain.

**And, in the rain,** I found the Raven.

He was in the act of stealing the sun, on a Tlingit Nation totem pole in front of the Tongass Historical Society Museum and Public Library. I stood by the totem pole and forgot about looking like a rubber duck. I grinned up at the Raven until the raindrops blotted my glasses. Then, in the raindrops' blur, I imagined he tipped his sharp-eyed glance at me for a second and winked.

Fine for you, I thought. You're smart. But *I* still can't remember the thing that bothered me at Mendenhall Glacier. In my memory of that icy episode, there's one chunk that's still frozen.

I removed my glasses, squinted at the Raven and sighed. "For the first time I sympathize with my family about the Sol's Salami jingle," I confided, shifting from thinking to muttering. "I go around the house singing it all the time. The jingle drives Mother and Madge crazy, cuz it gets stuck in their heads. Well, now this question is stuck in mine, and it's driving *me* crazy. *Why was Lavinia crabby?* What is it I'm not remembering?"

"What's this about Sol's Salami?" asked Madge, coming up behind me. She gave an elaborate shudder. "Surely we can be spared listening to that while we're on vacation...Do you know where Jack is?"

Madge was wearing an elegant, belted gray raincoat. A dark green scarf covered her head, then wound round her neck with the ends not showing at all. How *did* Madge always manage to look so tidy?

She caught me staring at her scarf. "*You* should think about headgear, Dinah. Your hair has frizzed into a giant cloud. Watch out! You'll probably get planes flying through it."

"Sorry, I can't hear you over the sound of your sweatshirt continuing to rip," I sniped back.

There came a weary "Girls..." from Mother, behind us, and we lapsed into a truce-like silence.

Mother wasn't the only one behind us. Other cabs had emptied out more *Empress Marie* passengers. Most of them immediately put up umbrellas. The effect was that the crowd rushing into the museum turned into a rainbow of circles rather than people.

Talbot St. John got out of a cab. He did a double-take at me. "Do you have something against rubber ducks?" I demanded — then an arm shot out from under a massive pink umbrella edged by large, plastic red roses and yanked him out of sight.

As Madge stepped round the totem pole, Jack jumped out at her. "Boo!"

*So* immature, I thought.

I must've been scowling, because Mother linked an arm through mine and soothed, "They won't be getting married any time soon, Dinah. I've told them they have to be well settled into their post-secondary courses — Jack at the University of British Columbia, Madge at Emily Carr — before they can even *think* about it."

"And at that point I hope you'll tell them to totally forget it," I said. "Statistics show —"

Mother cut me off hurriedly. "That's all right, dear. In an uncertain world, you can't blame people for wanting to secure the one thing they're sure of."

"What's that?"

"Love, of course," Mother said patiently.

I made loud retching noises. Together, we followed the last of the colorful circles into the museum.

**I met up with Raven** again in the Saxman Totem Park, three miles south of Ketchikan. The Tlingit park has the world's largest collection of freestanding totem poles. There were lots of Ravens, as well as, among others: eagles, which the Tlingit consider to be very spiritual; wolves, whose mask the headman of a clan will wear to show his leadership; and warriors, whose fierce, defiant features were earned in battle.

So Mother explained to us, reading out of a by now well-thumbed book on spirit legends. There are advantages to having a librarian as your maternal unit.

Walking around on my own, I forgot about other people. They just kind of faded. All I could see were the faces on the totem poles. The more I looked at them, the more they thrust themselves forward, looming at me one after another. But looming in a friendly way, if you know what I mean, even the warriors.

Madge must've felt the same, because, oblivious to the rain, she dropped her umbrella, pulled out her sketchbook and began drawing the faces. And this was someone who protected her hair at all costs from the tiniest drip. Eventually Jack noticed her getting soaked and hoisted the umbrella over her head while she worked.

Later, on a rare Good Samaritan impulse, I took over for him so he could wander around some more. I wheeled Madge into sketching a Raven face for me. I'd put it up in my room at home, beside my poster of Judy Garland belting out at Carnegie Hall.

"You've caught them perfectly," someone said, and we turned to see a woman with glossy black hair tucked into a cap. She smiled, displaying lots of laugh wrinkles. "The features in Tlingit art tend to be broad and bold, very distinctive."

There was something distinctive about the woman, too—distinctively familiar. I goggled at her before gasping out, "You're Elaine Hébert! Except for the cheerful expression, you look just like your stepsister."

The woman held out her hand. "Having heard what Julie's been up to, I'm semi-cheerful, at any rate. I'm sorry to intrude. I guessed you were the Galloway sisters; Captain Heidgarten told me you might be here. I wanted to thank you both. I understand that, because of you, we may be able to retrieve the mask."

"The particular Galloway you should thank would be my intrepid sister Dinah, not me," Madge said, shaking Elaine's hand.

I stopped gaping at Elaine long enough to demand, "Did the police catch Julie and Gooseberry Eyes?"

Elaine shrugged sadly. She also remained calm and nice when, in my excitement, I forgot to hold the umbrella straight and bonked her on the head with one of the spokes. "The police nabbed Julie, though they haven't recovered the mask yet. No sign of Julie's accomplice, either—er, Gooseberry Eyes."

Elaine sighed and looked even sadder, which made me feel twice as bad about bonking her on the head.

"I knew Julie was feeling bitter, but I didn't know how deep the bitterness went," Elaine confided. "You see, a couple of months ago, at Julie's insistence, I had an art-dealer friend assess Julie's paintings. Julie's been intense about her art for years, ever since our parents died. I think plunging into art was her way of blocking out the pain of only having known my dad and stepmother—her real mother—until she was age five. My own mom, who was divorced from my dad, raised us and, I'm afraid, always favored me.

"Anyhow, Julie had been begging me to invite him over, so I did. First she prepared dinner for all of us," Elaine explained. "Julie's pretty good in the kitchen—I'd finally convinced her to move in with me, out of her dingy apartment on Cadwallader, on the basis that she'd be earning her rent by cooking.

"Even a delicious meal couldn't soften the art dealer's opinion once he got a look at her paintings. His verdict was far different than Julie had hoped. He said she had little or no talent. Suggested, if she enjoyed painting, she keep it up as a hobby while she pursued something she was talented at, like cooking, or sports.

"He meant that, at least, as a compliment, but Julie was FURIOUS. Threw a tremendous tantrum in front of the art dealer and myself. Said I'd told the art dealer to find fault with her art so she wouldn't continue with it. And then—she trashed my house! A complete rampage. It was dreadful."

With the back of her palm, Elaine wiped away a tear. "Julie showed up the following afternoon at the Vancouver Roundhouse Community Center, where I was lecturing to a high school class, and—you'll never believe it—"

"Oh yes I will," I piped up. "She threw another tantrum. I know all about it."

Surprised, Elaine mustered a wan smile. "Well, Captain Heidgarten told me you were quite the sleuth, Dinah." She wiped some more tears away. "Anyhow, I thought a cruise would cheer Julie up, but it only seems to have inspired her to criminal scheming.

"And yet Julie has other, genuine talents. As I say, she's a wonderful cook and athlete. Maybe, with help, one day she'll learn to appreciate herself rather than trying to be something she's not."

With that pronouncement, Elaine broke into out-and-out sobbing. On a rare tactful impulse, I refrained from blurting out my next question, which was why Elaine had forbidden Julie to talk to people about the mask and about myths in general. If she wanted Julie to feel better about herself, why *not* let her do some public speaking or whatever?

Instead I thought about how Julie, that evening at our place, had remarked of the Raven: *I think if you were that clever, that capable of fooling others, it would be hard to stay on the straight and narrow all the time.*

Which, in a way, had been a confession, if only I'd listened more carefully. Julie thought *she* was Raven-clever—and had no intention of staying on the straight and narrow.

Madge was thinking about Julie too. She mused, "It's as if Julie has a warped mirror in her brain, which distorts her view of life."

"*Please*, Madge," I begged. "I want to know about Gooseberry Eyes."

Elaine shook her head. "Julie's accomplice got the wind up. The Blandish Arms Hotel concierge described a young man with pale-colored eyes who bolted when the police cruisers pulled up. Maybe the police will find the mask, eventually..."

Her voice trailed off, leaving a hopeless silence that only the patter of rain filled.

# Chapter 16

*Now you see Dinah—now you don't*

VANISHED, WITHOUT A TRACE!

Everyone stopped in front of the gigantic Hans and Roman poster before continuing on, with excited murmurs, into the ballroom where the two magicians would be performing. The poster showed them ushering a young woman into a large, upright coffin, then opening the coffin lid to reveal—nothing!

"I wish they could make some of these pounds vanish," remarked Madge, with a regretful glance down at her tummy. Which was, needless to say, flat and slim as ever.

"STUFF AND NONSENSE!" Ira Stone bellowed, dark eyes blazing.

Madge looked around, startled, but he was bellowing at Lavinia O'Herlihy. Ira was hobbling as fast as he could to outpace Lavinia; she was in grim pursuit.

"Stuff and nonsense. My sentiments exactly," Jack grinned. He lifted Madge's hand, which he was holding, and kissed it. "All we were eating was salmon, my vain one-and-only."

"Pounds and pounds of it," Madge mourned.

It was true. After touring the Saxman Totem Park, we'd sat down to a massive salmon feast in the Saxman Tribal Village. And I do mean massive. Ketchikan is known as the King Salmon Capital of the world; its peaceful waters teem with nummy fish.

I understood how Madge felt. I had tucked back so much I was practically sprouting gills.

Ahead of us, Lavinia clamped a blue-veined hand on one of Ira's stooped shoulders. "Trying to ditch me after all I've done for you," she scolded. Tightening her hold, she marched him on into the ballroom.

"Poor Ira," said Mother. "Lavinia's determined to snag him, no matter what. I bet he signed on for this cruise expecting it to be restful."

I giggled. "Maybe Hans and Roman will make Lavinia disappear," I suggested.

"She'd just faint," said Jack, wrinkling his freckled nose. No doubt he was remembering the dousing he'd received of Lavinia's perfume.

*Brrring!*

"My cell phone," Mother said in surprise. "I thought I'd turned it off. I didn't want it pealing out while Hans and Roman were busy extracting rabbits from hats."

She rummaged for the cell phone. This was just as much of a magic trick as anything Hans and Roman could do, the purse was so crammed.

I cleared my throat. "*I* switched the phone on, Mother. I left a message for Mr. Wellman."

"Hi, Mr. W.," Mother said into the phone. She gave it to me and warned, "Don't talk too long. If you come in after the lights go down, you won't be able to see us. And vice versa."

"I'll find you," I promised. "And no frantic signals to get my attention, Mother. It's so humiliating."

On the phone, my agent interrupted. "Dinah, keep in mind that I'm in my sixties now. I have only so much time left on this earth."

I backed against the wall, out of the stream of people. "Sorry, Mr. Wellman. I wanted to ask you a few questions about Julie Hébert."

Mr. Wellman's voice grew uneasy. "I heard a news report about theft, false identity, a police arrest and a lot of commotion in general, all to do with the *Empress Marie*. You wouldn't be involved in that commotion, would you, Dinah?"

"Heavily," I assured him. "But c'mon, Mr. Wellman. You spent time with Julie. Did she ever mention any friends

to you? I'm trying to figure out who Goose—who her accomplice is."

"Ah, accomplices. The plot thickens," said Mr. Wellman,
who, when he forgot to lecture his clients about being well-
behaved, had quite a touch of melodrama. "I never heard
her mention anyone, except Elaine. Hold on, though. The
one time I visited her at Elaine's house—what a messy
place, by the way!—Julie had a call on her cell. Answering
it, she said, 'Hi, Peabody.' *Peabody*!" Mr. Wellman laughed.
"Do you know, Mr. Peabody used to be a dog in a cartoon
I used to watch as a boy. Those were the days of great
animation, I tell—"

"Never mind about childhood nostalgia," I cut in rudely.
Honestly—grown-ups! "If Julie's caller was 'Peabody,' the
plot doesn't just thicken, it *cements*." I was remembering
the note in Mr. Trotter's side office, on top of the empty
file folder:

*Mr. Trotter—*

*Borrowed the contents of this for a while. Hope you*
*don't mind.*

*—Peabody Roberts*

"Peabody's the name of someone who works at Happy
Escapes Cruise Lines," I exclaimed. "I have to tell Mother
and Captain Heidgarten. Not to mention Mr. Trotter. His
mustache will probably fall right off! If only the Hans and
Roman show wasn't starting now..."

"Hans and Roman? Hey, I'd love to represent those two. Maybe you could approach 'em after the show and recommend Wellman Talent. You could..."

I placed the edge of a bitten-down fingernail on the cell's mouthpiece and scratched it back and forth. I was getting quite good at this. "Uh-oh, static, Mr. W. Bye now."

**What Mother had** warned me about had happened. I'd talked too long, and now the ballroom was dark. I stood helplessly inside the now closed double doors, unable to see anyone.

Anyone in the audience, that is. On a shimmering silver stage, Hans and Roman, in sequined tuxedos, were brandishing wands. Out of the wands' tips flew huge pink bubbles that bounced through the air and into the audience. Hans and Roman grinned above their pointy beards. In mid-air, the bubbles launching from the wands changed to blue.

Then Roman—I knew he was Roman because of the black R sewn on one of his sleeves—sneezed. "Uh-oh, I need a hanky," he proclaimed. He grabbed a passing bubble. It turned into a handkerchief the size of a mini-tablecloth! And, this being the *Empress Marie*, it was a blue mini-tablecloth with a fat white ship imprinted on it.

Applause and whistles. I forgot about worrying how to find Mother, Madge and Jack and joined in. Cool, I thought, and—*Hey, Dad, you should see this.*

Which is what I always think when something really special happens, though I never, never tell anyone.

Hans and Roman bowed. Then Hans, who had a big black H on *his* sleeve, announced: "And now it's time for our famous vanishing trick!" With his wand, he gestured at a large, upright silver coffin. "One lucky member of the audience gets to disappear, *poof!*" A swirl of smoke puffed from the tip of his wand. "No more creditors, no more taxes, no more mothers-in-law...at least until we magically bring you back, that is!"

Hans roared at his joke, but then hurried on as only very weak chuckles limped from the audience. "Er, yes. Well! Let's search for a victim—why, what am I saying? I mean, *volunteer*. Searchlights, please!"

Two silver orbs began gliding slowly over the audience. Spotting an anxious-faced Mother, along with Madge and Jack, near the stage, I waved to show her I was there.

Then I realized how useless this was. I was in pitch-darkness.

People were oohing and giggling. Who would be the victim/volunteer?

Somewhere beside me, one person wasn't oohing or giggling. I recognized a familiar whine.

"I waited and waited, and my relief person never showed up. The nerve!"

Fill-In, complaining again. Brother. She couldn't even relax long enough to enjoy a Hans and Roman show.

The spotlights shifted over more tables. There were Lavinia and the long-suffering Ira. Talbot and his sharp-faced mom. Evan. Mr. Trotter. Captain Heidgarten.

One of the spotlights moved, spilling on me. Hey, now Mother, Madge and Jack would see me! I waved to attract their notice.

Fill-In ranted on. "What I'm saying is, I waited, and the guy didn't appear. I was hopping mad!"

I kept waving, all the while glancing over the people in the other pool of silver light: Lavinia, Ira, Talbot and Sharp-Face, Evan, Mr. Trotter, Captain Heidgarten ...

The spotlight melted off them and fell on another group of tables.

"... waited and waited ... "

Roman boomed, "That girl waving at the back—we have a volunteer! An enthusiastic one, too. Strange. Usually we have to force someone to—er, I mean, how wonderful! Who *wouldn't* want to vanish courtesy of Hans and Roman? Why, I believe that's the *Empress Marie*'s singing sensation, Miss Dinah Galloway!"

I should have been thrilled that the famous Hans and Roman knew about me. But I was staring at the dark patch where the other spotlight had been.

Fill-In's words were echoing in my brain. *I waited and waited and the guy didn't show. The guy didn't show.*

The last frozen chunk of memory melted. I saw in my mind the Mendenhall Glacier Visitors' Center exactly the way I'd seen it through the binoculars.

And I knew, *I knew*, who Gooseberry Eyes was.

# Chapter 17

## Gooseberry Eyes, the less-than-ideal host

Gooseberry Eyes wasn't traveling by land. He'd hardly spent any time on land at all during this trip.

Gooseberry Eyes was here on the *Empress Marie*. Why hadn't I realized it before? Probably, dang it, because I'd liked the guy. He'd been here all along, and he was here now, in Hans and Roman's audience.

Well, if this audience liked surprises, it was in for a treat now. I sucked in a deep breath, preparing to belt out that I'd unmasked the mask thief. The applause was dying down; this was the perfect time.

Roman beckoned to me.

I opened my mouth—

A strong arm curved round my waist and hoisted me out of the spotlight.

"Bravo!" cried people from all over the ballroom. Even Fill-In stopped whining to exclaim, "*Remote* magic! I never!"

*I* never got to utter the faintest chirp. A hand muzzled my mouth, and I was whisked along the dark wall behind a row of tall, potted plants. Not that I could see the plants; I just felt their broad leaves brushing against me.

"Wait a minute," protested Hans and Roman, but applause overwhelmed them. Making someone disappear—without bothering to use their special magic coffin! What a triumph!

Meanwhile, my abductor opened a door behind the potted plants, whose thick leaves blocked the resulting wedge of light from the audience's view.

He whisked me through the door and beyond any possibility of help.


**"This is a service route,** you see," he panted, chuckling. He bore me down a long white corridor that soon bent into an even longer downward slope. "Very busy in the daytime, don't you know. But rarely during showtime. No calls for room service—our clients are occupied with the quality acts we book. Alas, the curtain is about to come down a bit early on one of those acts. The loudest one, our singing star, Dinah Galloway."

I'd been kicking fiercely; that hadn't deterred him. So instead I chomped down hard on the palm of his hand.

"OW!" Gratifyingly, he removed his hand and stopped to shake the feeling back into it.

"Let me just see your gooseberry eyes, Gooseberry Eyes," I said. Reaching up with both hands, I stretched his eyelids way to the sides. A dark-tinted contact lens sprang out of each eye. I plucked off the bushy white wig, too, while I was at it.

"You're too young for Lavinia," I observed as gooseberry eyes blinked at me in surprise from wrinkled folds of skin. Makeup-wrinkled folds of skin. Close up, I saw that now. "You should have stayed at the Happy Escapes office, Peabody Roberts, instead of sneaking aboard the *Empress Marie* in an old man's disguise. And Lavinia should have enjoyed her afternoon at Mendenhall Glacier instead of storming about, fuming, because you'd disappeared. To sneak up the trail and push me in the lake, I might add."

Peabody Roberts gave a dry giggle, like the sound of dead leaves being stepped on and crushed. "You might, indeed!"

"And you're definitely old enough to know better than to steal," I continued.

I didn't wait for a reply. Instead, I began to yell.

"That won't do you any good at all," Peabody snapped. "The walls are solid—to protect our precious passengers from being disturbed by the jangle of room-service trolleys."

I ceased yelling. It was time to breathe, anyway. "How *did* you manage to sneak aboard as Ira Stone?" I demanded.

Peabody retrieved the wig and stuffed it into my mouth. Then, clutching me closer, he resumed scuttling down the long slope. "I borrowed the passenger list from Trotter. Wanted to see who'd canceled. Whose place I could take. It was Julie's idea."

He giggled again. "It was Julie who got me hired on as a summer student. Julie, forging her famous sister Elaine's name on the recommendation letter. Hee-hee!"

Peabody was panting again, but evidently the pleasure of bragging was worth the discomfort of talking while he hurried. And got kicked. "Ow! Now cut that out...I stayed after hours one day, logged on to Trotter's computer and, on the master passenger list, changed *Stone, Ira* from cancelled to confirmed."

"Mmmflgtch," I commented, and I landed a good kick on Peabody's shins.

"OWWW! C'mon now. My back is still sore from falling down along with your crummy trellis. What's the matter with your family, can't they afford decent building materials?" Peabody complained.

We reached the bottom of the slope. Peabody paused, his free hand on the doorknob. "You're probably wondering how I got Ira Stone's passport," he smirked. "Broke into the old geezer's house. He's in the hospital—that's why he canceled out on the cruise. I got his American Express card, too!

"At the terminal, you thought I'd left—but I changed into my old-man duds in the stairwell and hobbled aboard as Ira. Sweet, huh?"

"Mmmflgtch!"

"Thank you," Peabody said modestly. He swung the door open and we passed into a hallway with stateroom doors on both sides—but, sadly for me, with no one going in or out of them.

As Peabody had said, everyone was at the show.

**Peabody stumbled into** his stateroom, or rather Ira Stone's, and sank back against the door, panting anew. I wrenched myself loose and I sprinted for the phone—but never made it. Peabody hoisted me again.

"One thing you have to say for thieves," he smirked. "We stay in good shape."

He bore me out to the balcony.

Balcony! I forgot to yell for the moment. I hadn't been on an *Empress* balcony before. How nice it would be to sit out here, well bundled up, of course, with a steaming mug of hot chocolate, under the glittery stars and yellow, buttery moon.

Somehow I didn't think a nice evening was what Peabody had in mind. A considerate host would not, for example, be dangling his guest over the balcony's edge. And giggling while he did so.

I was shaking all over. "You won't get away with this," I chattered through my nervously hip-hopping teeth. A clichéd observation, to be sure, but wit and originality seemed to have fled.

"Oh yes I will," Peabody giggled. "Julie got busted, but I'm free as a bird—ha! free as the *Raven* bird. That idiot Trotter will never get the hint about who I am. And that old hag Lavinia—I told her the only way I'd consider marrying her is if she stopped jabbering about the guy who crashed into her at the terminal. I told her if there was one thing I couldn't stand, it was a whiner. That's why Lavinia clammed up about Gooseberry Eyes. By the way, that's not a very flattering nickname," he added, pouting.

Great. A villain with hurt feelings. "What do you want, a written apology?" I chattered.

"Hee-hee! Always with the wisecracks! But you see what I mean? Julie always said *she* was as smart as the Raven. Turns out I'm the one who is! There's no evidence against me, no evidence at all!"

He giggled yet again, a habit that was really starting to grate on me.

"*I'm* evidence," I snapped.

Probably not the wisest remark to make, in the circumstances.

"There is no you, not anymore," Peabody pointed out.

And dropped me into the ocean.

# Chapter 18
## The unexpected rescuer

Cartwheeling down, I went in left elbow first. The cold SMACK of the waves was so fierce that I couldn't breathe. I could only stare hopelessly up at the fat white bar of soap, which the *Empress Marie* resembled more than ever through my blurry, sopping glasses. The *Empress* was moving briskly by and would soon sail beyond me. It's at night that cruise ships pick up their speed.

I gasped hoarsely and finally took something in — a huge mouthful of icy seawater. Coughing it out, I yelled, "HELP!"

And went under. Till then, without realizing it, I'd been treading water. Round, flat, rhythmic strokes, just as Jack had taught me.

Now, panicking, I reverted to my old, pre-lessons, freaking-out ways. I chopped and thrashed at the water while gasping with fright.

And sank under a huge black wave.

Down, down it pushed me. I couldn't swim; no point in trying. I was going numb. In a second I'd see Dad again, with his black eyes bright and full of life. Maybe this time he'd actually play me a Peggy Lee song.

Because this time I knew "Is That All There Is?" was my song, all right. That's all there was going to be for me.

I saw Dad—but he wasn't smiling and reaching for an album to play. He was saying, *C'mon, you gotta try harder than that. What did Jack teach you?*

I pushed myself up through the waves and forced my limbs into the strokes I'd learned. Forced them pretty clumsily at first, but I bobbed into place on the water's surface. I surfed the waves instead of being rolled by them.

But the fat white bar of soap was streaming on by. Even through my watery glasses I could see the stern approaching.

*Your voice, Dinah! You've got this great gift,* Dad would say to me. He'd add teasingly, *This great LOUD gift.* Only now, he was speaking impatiently.

*Your voice, darlin'. It'll save you.*

My voice had saved me in the past. Once I'd been able to summon help while trapped in a broom closet; once I'd prevented a jewel thief from escaping a crowded theater.

Three times not lucky. My throat was swollen and dry from the salt. My limbs needed all the energy I could muster to keep treading water. "I...can't," I croaked.

The stern was almost alongside me. No one would see. No one would hear.

*Sure they will, kid.*

"They won't," I croaked and started to cry. "Dad..."

Then, incredibly, I heard my voice belting out into the night.

**A face appeared** in a porthole. "Help!" I gasped. Since there was minuscule volume attached to my voice, this plea for help went nowhere. I raised an arm in a frantic wave. Which ruined my semi-smooth strokes, and I sank.

I emerged, hacking out my latest intake of salt water. The face was still there! I squinted through my blurred lenses. The face was—*it was looking down at me!*

"DINAH!" bellowed Talbot St. John. "OH GOD, *DINAH!* STAY THERE—I'LL GET HELP!"

**"Stay there?!"** I regarded Talbot shakily over the largest mug of hot chocolate I'd ever seen, plus folds and folds of the snug blue-and-white blankets I was wrapped in. "So you're a comedian as well as a lifesaver."

Used to insults from me, Talbot looked at me uncertainly from under his dark, soulful forelock of hair. But then I grinned, and he grinned back.

We were in the lounge where I sang every evening. It had been converted to a sort of emergency center. The emergency being, as far as I could tell, which adult could fuss over me the most. Dozens of them were milling around us, including, also wrapped in blankets, the two stewards who'd jumped in after me with life preservers when Talbot pulled the emergency alarm; the officer who'd let down the emergency ladder for us to climb; and Captain Heidgarten, Mother, Madge, Jack—oh, the list went on and on. All these grown-ups fussing and fuming and, in my mother's and sister's cases, closer to drowning in tears than I'd been in the ocean.

I ignored them. They had other stuff to talk about, anyway; namely, where was Peabody Roberts? The noise of my rescue—that is, the prolonged, frantic screams from onlookers—had alerted him to hide. The Coast Guard had even come aboard to help with the search.

"You saved me," I marveled. I still couldn't believe it. After all, I'd almost drowned—but I wouldn't think about that now. Another time.

More fun to watch Talbot blush with embarrassment. Apparently he'd been about to jump in himself, until another steward forcibly restrained him. *Whaddya think that is down there, a convention?* the steward had barked.

Mother, who was speaking through her sobs of relief to Captain Heidgarten, glanced tearily over at me. From her expression I could tell she was about to swoop down on me for the trillionth time with hugs. Ditto Madge.

"Let's go sit near Evan," I murmured to Talbot. "If Madge says to me one more time that she's never going to find me annoying again, I'll be ill. I mean, we're *sisters*."

I clutched my blankets around me and followed Talbot to the piano, where Evan was tinkling out his *dah DAH dah dah DAH dah* tune. "Don't even think about hugging me," I warned him. "You've had two bear ones already, so you've used up your quota."

Evan laughed. "I'm busy being in shock over your chatting in an apparently civilized fashion with Talbot...Dah DAH dah dah DAH dah," he crooned.

Talbot and I pulled up chairs behind him. "The weird thing," I confided to Talbot, "was that I could have sworn I heard myself singing. But it was impossible. I had no voice at all."

The *Empress Marie*'s head chef bustled up to us with a tray of fresh chocolate chip cookies, the chips so hot they were still dripping, and two tall glasses of cold milk. About every ten minutes the chef was showing up with more food.

"I'll have to go overboard more often," I joked.

The chef removed his towering white hat and began weeping into it. "Don't say that," he begged. "When I think of you in those dark, churning waves—!" He rushed out, his roly-poly frame trembling with emotion.

Talbot raised a glass of milk to me in salute. "You *were* hearing yourself, Dinah. It wasn't impossible. I—well, I have this CD of yours. Of yours and the rest of the cast of *The Moonstone*, I mean. I was playing the track where you sing "Blue Moon," and it was so moving I stuck my head out the porthole to see the real moon. Which is how I spotted you. So," he finished, offering me the tray, "in a way you rescued yourself."

"That's much too noble of you, Talbot," I said. "Why not claim credit? I do, whenever possible. But hold on. You were listening to me? I thought you found me loud. As in, LOUD," I corrected, remembering the conversation I'd overheard between him and Liesl.

"I do," Talbot said enthusiastically. "I love loud. Er, LOUD. I have all these old albums of great belter-outers like Bessie Smith, Ethel Waters, Judy Garland, Sarah Vaughan... and now you," he added shyly. "My dad and I saw you in *The Moonstone* last fall. He's the one who introduced me to jazz and swing music. I've wanted to tell you how much I thought of you, except..."

Except I've gone out of my way to ignore you, I thought. I just assumed you were a snob because Liesl Dubuque hung around you all the time, and *she's* one.

I began to see that masks weren't only put on by those wearing them. Sometimes people created masks that, in their minds, they put on *other* people. Masks that were their own wrong ideas about the other people. I'd put such a mask on Talbot.

"I did hear you tell Liesl the Weasel that I was enough to break the sound barrier," I pointed out.

"Huh?" Talbot's deep brown eyes were puzzled. Then his face cleared. "Ah, pre-brussels sprout attack, you mean. No, I was trying to shake Liesl off. She kind of trails after me like an extra shadow." Talbot grimaced. "Even e-mails me all the time—it's to the point where I delete her messages without reading 'em. Anyhow, that one evening I was starting to tell her off. To note that, speaking of breaking the sound barrier, *her* shrill tones would probably be able to crack it wide open. But then the volley of brussels sprouts began, and..."

I wrapped the blankets over my head. "I am sooo sorry," I said in anguished, muffled tones. "I didn't know. Please forgive me." For more than you know, I thought. For even thinking at one point you might have shoved me into Mendenhall Lake!

"Friends tend to forgive," Talbot returned. He chuckled, a nice, humorous-sounding chuckle not at all like Peabody's dead-leaves one. "Besides, it wasn't like you were throwing bricks or anything."

"I'd like to meet your dad sometime," I said, still too chagrined to emerge from under the blankets.

"Well, you have, Dinah. He's been with you for the whole cruise. Haven't you, Dad?"

"You bet," came Evan's voice.

# Chapter 19

*The end of Lavinia's courtin' days*

I was still absorbing the news about Evan and Talbot the next morning when Peabody Roberts, a.k.a. Gooseberry Eyes, was caught.

He'd eluded the *Empress Marie*'s crew and members of the Coast Guard right up till we docked in Juneau, our last stop before heading home. It was a maid who found Peabody, hiding under a jumble of sheets and towels in a hamper.

"Talk about airing the ship's dirty laundry," growled Captain Heidgarten as several Coast Guard officers hauled Peabody along the main deck.

I elbowed Evan. "Why didn't you tell me you were Talbot's dad?" I demanded. It was all very exciting about Peabody, but, as Mother and Madge often say, when I get a bee in my bonnet, it's a queen bee. That is, I become a royal pain until I've had my curiosity satisfied.

"You said you couldn't stand Talbot. You didn't want to see him on the cruise," Evan replied, wincing as Peabody squirmed to get loose and was gripped more tightly by his captors.

"Pardon me," I said, "but is your name not Evan *Brander*?"

Evan grinned. " 'Evan Brander' is my stage name. Brander is actually my middle name. No way any self-respecting musician is going to appear onstage with the moniker 'St. John.' Too pretentious-sounding!"

"Not to me," I said—and it wasn't, not now that I knew Talbot, and not ever again.

I thought of the satisfying game of backgammon Talbot and I had already played that morning. The early game, since I'd had bad dreams all night. Talbot had been glad to play; he was an early riser.

I had a feeling I was going to be an early riser for a while too. In the daytime you can postpone horrible images, like icy black waves and blurry white ships that float out of reach. In the nighttime, dreams aren't so cooperative.

I changed subjects. "But how come you were prowling around Julie's room so much? I thought maybe you were after the mask."

"Good Lord!" exclaimed Evan, trading startled looks with Talbot. "Nothing quite so diabolical, Dinah-Mite. Our stateroom is in that hall, next to Julie's. I was afraid that if I continued past her door to my own, and opened it, you'd glimpse Tal and be upset. I was also worried about that when he and I went to Mendenhall Glacier—though it turned out you had far more serious distractions to deal with there."

"I'm upset at *myself*," I moaned. So often in life I searched for complicated answers when there were simple ones handy. Come to think of it, Talbot's was the voice I'd heard when the steward knocked on the door for room service. I was dumb, *dumb*, DUMB.

I clutched my hair. I'd washed it that morning, and Madge, overcoming strong objections from me, had actually brushed it out—revealing, astoundingly, a burnished red color only a smidgen lighter than her own. Wow! I might use a brush myself, every few months or so.

The brisk wind was fast whirling my hair into untidiness again, and of course my grabbing it by the ends didn't help.

"Yes, *completely* uncontrolled, I'd say," snapped a voice down at the far end of the deck.

It was the disapproving tanned, middle-aged woman. I jumped, probably because my nerves were still edgy. After the previous night's experience, I figured they'd settle down in, oh, about forty years. I jarred Talbot's hand, which happened to be holding a jumbo bag of ketchup-flavored potato chips—his *and* my favorite chip flavor, it turned out.

Chips poured over the railing to flutter onto the heads of the people on the deck below. I yelped with laughter.

Talbot, however, immediately got a solemn, conscientious look on his face and said he'd better go down and apologize.

"Don't be ridiculous," I scoffed. Obviously this boy needed to be taken under my wing and trained.

There would be lots of time for that, because we were discussing the idea of forming a musical group, along with Pantelli. Talbot played guitar, electric guitar and drums; Pantelli was a piano prodigy; and of course I could supply the pipes. The only challenge would be wrenching Pantelli away from his tree studying, but we could always remind him that ebonies and ivories were made of wood.

Anyhow, that was for the future. Right now, Peabody was being dragged along in front of us. "*You*," he snarled at me. "You were supposed to disappear."

Reaching for a potato chip, I crunched into it as loudly as possible. "I always come back for encores," I informed him loftily.

Farther along, the middle-aged woman continued to rant to her companion, who was wearing a floppy pink straw hat. Lavinia!

"Goodness knows, I've certainly tried to enjoy this cruise," the middle-aged woman said. "However, a sandy-haired young man keeps playing practical jokes on me. Told me first that he was planning to marry a young girl and then *you*, an old lady!"

Lavinia drew back, offended. "I'm not that old," she harrumphed. "Anyhow, I am planning to marry."

"Well, I hope it's someone your own age. I've had enough of these distasteful jokes."

"Oh, Ira is most definitely my age. A few years senior, perhaps."

Evan, Talbot and I exchanged amused glances. Evidently news of Ira/Gooseberry Eyes/Peabody's capture hadn't quite got round to everyone.

The Coast Guard officers hauled Peabody along, and the next moment he and they were beside the middle-aged woman and Lavinia.

Leaning forward, I saw Peabody's long, thin profile twisting into a sneer. "Hi, Lavvy baby," he jeered. "Don't you recognize your darling Ira? So when will our wedding bells ring, toots?"

Lavinia swayed and had to clutch the railing.

"I don't believe it!" the middle-aged woman spat at her. "You, as well!"

And she stalked off.

# Chapter 20
## The Raven and the songbird

Talbot and I headed off to play volleyball. "You're much too nice," I lectured him. "That's why you haven't been able to shake Liesl the Weasel."

"Oh yeah? Here's a not-nice shot for you, kiddo." He lobbed a high one.

"Dang! It's the late birthday curse," I lamented, having leaped for it in vain. "Someday I'll be tall like Madge. You wait!"

"Madge? Is that your sister?"

"Yeah." I frowned at him. "You saw her at the Totem Park, remember? She was beside me when I was in yellow duck mode."

"I saw you," Talbot shrugged. "I didn't notice her."

I dropped the ball, which I'd been about to serve. A male of the species—*not noticing Madge?!*

"Let me get this straight," I said feebly. "You noticed me and not my sister?"

"Yeah. So?" Talbot's brown eyes were puzzled. "What's the big deal, Dinah?"

"Ohhh…nothing. Just that my nerves will now be in shock for another *eighty* years."


**But where was** the Raven? A search of Peabody's room had yielded lists of wealthy art collectors he'd been busy contacting; tins of the thick, gooey makeup he'd been wearing; sets of false, wobbly, old men's teeth—

"That explains the clicking thing he was doing with his mouth." Madge shuddered. "He had to keep pushing the teeth back into place."

No Raven, though. Elaine, who'd flown down to Juneau at the news of Peabody's arrest, looked rather despairingly at Captain Heidgarten. We were all in his office, watching the spindly hands on his brass clock tick on and on. In the evening the *Empress Marie* would pull out of Juneau, and the Heritage Gallery still would not have its mask.

Elaine had cleared up one mystery, at any rate. As soon as she found out Gooseberry Eyes' identity, she buried her face in her hands. "Not Peabody. Not *Peebles*," she moaned. "He's the high school friend Julie always told me about. The unpleasant prankster who let air out of the tires of teachers' cars when he didn't like his marks. Who dumped garbage on the lawns of kids who made fun of his clumsiness in gym class. Julie laughed at his pranks, comparing him to the tricky Raven. I refused to let her bring Peebles to the house. I'd heard too many bad things about him.

"I was so relieved when he and his parents moved back to Alaska—and so disappointed when I recently heard he was back in Vancouver. Such a bad influence on Julie!"

I didn't point out that Julie herself was hardly the type to exert a Mother Teresa-like influence. Instead I repeated "Peebles?" and from somewhere I heard the gentle click of a jigsaw puzzle piece falling into place. "I get it. 'Peebles' is Peabody's nickname. You told Julie not to talk to *Peebles*, not people, about the mask."

"When Julie persisted in her friendship with Peabody, I'm afraid I lost my temper with her. Told her she knew nothing about people." Elaine shook her head.

"Maybe our first theory was correct," Captain Heidgarten was commenting thoughtfully. "Maybe Peabody did stow the Raven somewhere on land."

"I dunno," Jack said. "A priceless mask isn't exactly the type of thing you stuff in a public locker."

Talbot was sitting just outside the office's open door, on the *Empress Marie*'s suggestion box. Mr. Trotter, who kept dabbing at his forehead with an *Empress Marie* hanky, had told Talbot he could only stand to be with one kid in a small, enclosed space at a time. "The Captain's cabin isn't small," Talbot had argued—but, polite as he was, he stepped out and switched on his CD player.

Now he piped up, in the unnaturally loud voice you tend to use when wearing headphones, "PEABODY LUGGED—sorry. Peabody, in his Ira disguise, lugged a huge shopping bag back on board the *Empress* after our first visit to Juneau. Myra and I were right behind him. I offered to help him carry it, but he just shouted, 'STUFF AND NONSENSE!' and scuttled away from me. Betcha the mask was in the shopping bag."

"Since he'd grabbed it that morning in his thief disguise." I nodded. "Yup, it's gotta be aboard."

The "Myra" Talbot had referred to was the sharp-faced woman who'd been accompanying him on excursions. She wasn't his mother at all—his mom was at home, as Evan had once told me, with a wee daughter. Myra was an assistant of Mr. Trotter's, an official companion to under-aged tourists.

Mr. Trotter was regarding Talbot with pursed lips, as if there were an extremely bad odor sitting outside on the suggestion box, rather than a twelve-year-old boy. "This whole episode has been so distressing," he mourned, patting his mustache. "Imagine—Peabody Roberts! He seemed so quiet. So well-behaved. Just what we like at Happy Escapes. Though he did rip off my egg sandwich—that I'll never forgive," the program director said darkly, as if this were a far worse crime than ripping off the Raven.

Captain Heidgarten sighed. "Dinah, was there anything at all Julie or Peabody said that referred to the Raven's whereabouts?"

I'd thought about this myself, endlessly. "Mostly Julie and Peabody were congratulating themselves on how clever they were," I said. "Julie had this fascination with how clever the Raven was—she was sure she'd out-clevered him with her schemes."

*Those fools haven't the faintest hint*, Julie had laughed into her cell phone.

Captain Heidgarten and Mr. Trotter then got into a debate about whether the passengers' staterooms should be searched for the mask. The program director was indignant at the idea; the more he argued, the more he sweated, which made his mustache ends droop inch by inch.

"HEY, DINAH—er, sorry. Hey, Dinah," said Talbot. He beckoned to me, and, glad to escape the rising tempers, I joined him outside the door.

He placed the headphones over my ears. "Get a load of this. It's a compilation of stuff Dad and I burned on a CD. You were asking about Peggy Lee—here she is."

Peggy's velvety tones poured into my ears: "Is that all there is?" I could see why Dad liked her. Mellow and moody! A hint of mischief as well. *That* would've appealed to him especially.

A hint of mischief.

Hint.

That word was coming up a lot lately. Julie, with her *Those fools haven't the slightest hint*. And Peabody, giggling, *That idiot Heidgarten will never get the hint!*

"Is that all there is?" crooned Peggy.

"YEAH, THAT IS ALL THERE IS," I said slowly. Or shouted slowly. I removed the headphones and lowered my voice. "All there is, is a hint," I announced to everyone. "That's all we need."

By now the program director's mustache was hanging straight down, he was sweating so badly. "I'll tell you what *I* need," he fumed. "A long, *long* vacation. I—"

"Just a minute, Lionel," Captain Heidgarten interrupted. "I think I espy a large light bulb switching on above our sensational singing redhead. Dinah?"

"I know where the Raven is," I gulped. "Talbot's sitting on it."

"Huh?" Talbot leaped off the suggestion box as if it had suddenly caught fire.

The, pardon me, Happy Escapes Helpful Hints suggestion box.

**The Raven grinned** up at us from his bed of dozens of Helpful Hints suggestion forms. He was radiantly red, bold, bright—and cleverer than Julie and Peabody after all. He'd be going home to the Juneau Heritage Gallery, and they'd be going to jail.

Not that Julie and Peabody hadn't been clever to come

up with the Helpful Hints suggestion box as a hiding place. The box was the one spot nobody checked on until after the end of a cruise—and Peabody, with the key he'd filched from the Happy Escapes office, had put the Raven inside, intending to remove it as soon as he found a buyer in Alaska. Then, still in his Ira Stone disguise, he'd return to Vancouver a much wealthier man, and no one the wiser.

Now I grinned back at the Raven. He always made me grin. I thought, *Hey, Dad, you should see this!*

Elaine hugged me. "Thank you so much, Dinah! You *found* him!"

I was growing pretty Raven-red myself. "It's okay," I mumbled as everyone crowded around. "It's—" What could I say? I hated this kind of thing.

Then I remembered what Talbot had said to *me*. "It's what friends do for each other," I told Elaine.

**Talbot and I ran** into the lounge, where Evan was tinkling out his *Dah DAH dah dah DAH dah* number.

"We got the mask!" we yelled.

"No, *I* got the mask," Evan said happily. "It's been right in my face the whole trip. Y'know, the mask this, the mask that, and I didn't get it till just now."

Talbot raised his eyebrows at me. "Uh, sorry, Dinah, musicians are a bit eccentric sometimes…"

"Listen, guys," glowed Evan. "It's Dah DAH dah dah DAH dah no more."

He began to play and sing:

*The mask on the cruise ship*
*The stranger at sea—*
*Is it my true love,*
*Waiting for me?*

*Ms. X. on the ocean*
*Too shy to reveal*
*Her name, her face, yet*
*Love's what I feel.*

Love, I thought. Trust a grown-up! But I quite liked the song. Love wasn't so bad. Maybe I'd give Madge and Jack some slack. A teeny amount, anyway.

"Why don't we practice it together?" I suggested to Evan. "I'll sing it tonight."

He beamed. "I'd be honored. What a friend!"

I turned to Talbot, who was beaming as well. "Er, Talbot. About friendship. What you said, that friends tend to forgive each other."

"Yeah, definitely they do."

"Um…" Now that the end of the cruise was drawing near, I was picturing Liesl Dubuque's sharp, and very likely furious, face under her newly close-cropped hair. A face that would all too soon be thrusting itself into mine—and screaming abuse.

I said, "I was wondering if, well, if you could sort of promise me in advance one more forgiveness. You know, like Club Z points against a purchase."

Talbot stared at me from beneath his dark forelock of hair that no longer seemed the slightest bit soulful or silly to me. It was just him. "Sure. I guess. I don't exactly—"

"Would you promise, though? One free forgiveness?"

"Uh, okay. You got it." Then, abruptly, he grinned at me. "You're one of a kind, Dinah Galloway."

Which he could have meant as an insult, but somehow I didn't think so. In fact, I felt very happy all of a sudden. Raven-happy. Sometimes the Raven did good things, and sometimes not so good at all, but he loved life with an enthusiasm as bright as the sun he stole for Earth.

Hey, this love stuff was making more and more sense—and especially, as Mother had said, in an uncertain world.

"I'd love to do your song," I told Evan. "Let's try it right now!"

*Hey, Dad...*

# The Spy in the Alley
# A Dinah Galloway Mystery
# Melanie Jackson

Meet Dinah Galloway: eleven years old, headstrong and impulsive, with a voice that can raise the roof and an appetite to match. Confronting a prowler in the backyard, Dinah is determined to find out why someone has taken an interest in her older sister and herself. Who is the bucktoothed burglar? Why are the Rinaldis' tomatoes always involved? And what is the connection between Madge's boyfriend and GASP, a group of well-intentioned anti-smoking activists?

Dinah gets by on pluck, courage and an irrepressible sense of humor as she is catapulted into a mystery that twists and turns from the blackberry patch to the corporate boardroom.

1-55143-207-2 • $8.95 CDN • $6.95 US

# The Man in the Moonstone
## A Dinah Galloway Mystery
## Melanie Jackson

Dinah Galloway, fresh from her adventures with spies and bucktoothed burglars, is back in a hilarious new adventure.

Chosen for a lead role in the musical version of Wilkie Collins' *The Moonstone*, eleven-year-old Dinah – amateur detective, budding singer and unabashed owner of a huge appetite – is once again embroiled in a mystery that puts her in peril and offers plenty of opportunities for humor and good food.

Assisted by her long-suffering friend and ardent tree lover, Pantelli, and her overprotective, glamorous older sister, Madge, Dinah brings down the house in this second installment of the Dinah Galloway mystery series.

1-55143-264-1 • $8.95 CDN • $6.95 US